KISSING KATE

"I think we should watch the game," Kate said, but she made no effort to move.

Alex stroked the back of her neck gently, sending another shiver rippling through her. "I think you should kiss me. Or I can kiss you. Either way, there should be kissing."

"Alex . . ."

"You said that already. Give me something else. Anything, Red. Honestly, I'll let you talk me out of this if you try. But I'm a competitive man, and right now the win is in sight, and damn"—he bit his lip as his gaze dropped back down to her mouth—"I want the win."

"I'm not willing to be one of many."

"No one is asking you to be. I'm just asking you to wait for me. Spend time with me now; we'll keep it easy and casual. Do whatever you like, whenever you like."

"So you're saying you're keeping your vow of celibacy, but you want to hang out with me. And only me?"

"Plus kissing."

A grin played at her lips. "Plus kissing. And if I say yes, what then?" The words were breathy and full of meaning. She was asking what their next step would be.

"I don't know. All I know is that if I don't kiss you now, I'm going to go crazy."

"So kiss me."

"Yeah?"

"Kiss me . . ."

Books by Melissa West

Racing Hearts

Wild Hearts

Published by Kensington Publishing Corporation

WILD HEARTS

A Hamilton Stables Novel

Melissa West

LYRICAL SHINE
Kensington Publishing Corp.
www.kensingtonbooks.com

LYRICAL SHINE BOOKS are published by

Kensington Publishing Corp.
119 West 40th Street
New York, NY 10018

All Kensington titles, imprints, and distributed lines are available at special quantity discounts for bulk purchases for sales promotion, premiums, fund-raising, educational, or institutional use.

Special book excerpts or customized printings can also be created to fit specific needs. For details, write or phone the office of the Kensington Sales Manager: Kensington Publishing Corp., 119 West 40th Street, New York, NY 10018. Attn. Sales Department. Phone: 1-800-221-2647.

LYRICAL Shine and the Lyrical Shine logo are trademarks of Kensington Publishing Corp.

First Electronic Edition: February 2016
eISBN-13: 978-1-61650-827-2
eISBN-10: 1-61650-827-2

First Print Edition: February 2016
ISBN-13: 978-1-61650-828-9
ISBN-10: 1-61650-828-0

Printed in the United States of America

For my first and last love, Jason.

ACKNOWLEDGMENTS

A million thanks to God for guiding me each day.

Thank you to my amazing agent, Nicole Resciniti, and my fantastic editor, John Scognamiglio, for helping make this book what it is today. Also, thank you to Rebecca Cremonese and the rest of the staff at Kensington for being so wonderful!

A big thank you to my husband, Jason, and my two daughters for putting up with me when I'm on deadline. And thank you to the rest of my amazing family and friends for your support and love.

Thank you to Rachel Harris and Staci Murden for reading early versions of this book and being amazing friends. Also, I could not write without the support and friendship of Cindi Madsen. I adore you.

Finally, thank YOU for reading this book, for reading all books, and for continually supporting the writing and reading communities. We could not do this without you!

Chapter One

Alex Hamilton groaned as he rolled over in bed, the taste of gin still on his lips, his throat cottony from a hangover he couldn't afford to have. A manufactured floral scent floated in the air, and his stomach roiled. Cursing himself, he sat up and immediately groaned again at the ringing in his ears and the pain slicing through the center of his brain. Why the hell did he drink? He'd asked himself that single question on more occasions than he could count, each one with the same answer—no damn clue. And no damn sense.

Pushing out of his sheets, he stood, stretching his long and lean body until the joints in his back cracked, then started for the shower as his foot hit a pair of boots on the floor. Boots that weren't his and weren't men's, for that matter. He lifted one very tall black boot into the air, curious how anyone managed to walk on such a high heel but being thankful all the same, because damn, he loved a woman in knee-high boots. All this went through his mind without much thought still as to who the boots belonged to, until he heard someone clearing her throat from behind him. Shit. *Please tell me she isn't still in my—*

"Good morning, handsome."

Dammit.

Alex turned slowly to find a very blond woman in his bed. She couldn't be more than five two or so, had golden tan skin, and the sort of face that never much needed makeup, yet she slathered it on all the same. Black splotches covered her under eyes from mascara or liner or whatever the hell women put on their eyes. She looked young— too young really. Young enough that he wondered if he'd ever stopped to ask her age.

As though she read his thoughts, she stepped out of the bed, not caring to cover her naked body, which didn't sit well with Alex. There was once a time when he would have appreciated such audacity, but that time had long since come and gone. He missed female modesty and soft smiles, the looks and actions of a Southern lady. The kind of lady his mother would have liked if she were still alive. And in two years he'd only been with one woman who met that description, but she'd walked away, or maybe he'd walked away. Still, over a year later he wasn't sure which of them had actually left.

But taking in the woman before him, Alex found her nakedness grated on his nerves. Of course he, too, stood with nothing on, and feeling a tinge of unease about that fact, he crossed his arms over his chest and stared at the woman.

Her gaze dipped down to his lower half, still very exposed despite the whole crossing-his-arms thing. "It's Brittany, and I'm twenty-two," she said, bouncing with each word, a triumphant smile on her face.

Alex almost laughed, unsure if he should congratulate her or show her out. He'd never heard someone reveal her age with such pride. Again, he wondered what the hell he was doing. He had to be at the foaling barn in an hour, and knowing his brother, he was already—

Before he could finish his thought, his cell vibrated against the nightstand. He glanced over, not wanting to take the call in front of the girl, but then he caught Trip's name flashing across the screen. Not answering would only result in another call, which made Alex wonder if Trip managed the whole farm in this obsessive way or just him? Something told him it was just him.

"Look," he said to Brittany, "I hate to play and run, but I've got a busy schedule and—" The phone vibrated again, supporting his story.

"Play and run? You've got to be kidding me." She grabbed up her clothes and jerked her dress down over her body, hopping as she pulled on her boots. "Play and run! Who even says that? I'll see my-self out." Then she stopped at the door and spun around. "And when Trip asks why I quit, just let him know I refused to work with his jackass of a brother."

She slammed the door shut and Alex cringed, searching his mind for a Brittany who worked at the farm, and that was when he remembered his conversation with Trip the week before. New exercise rider Brittany Light. Well, there went that.

Taking his phone from his nightstand, he texted his brother that he'd see him in twenty, then jumped in the shower to wash off his night, his thoughts on the week he had before him. Calls with two stud farms, vet checks on the broodmares, and hopefully a flight out to Ireland later in the week to buy a new stallion.

And he still hadn't made the decision everyone was waiting on him to make—choosing the studs for the McKendricks' broodmares. He had two perfectly good options in his stallion barn, ready to go, one already producing champions, so what was the problem? The problem was that he'd long since known that breeding was less science, more art, and he was close to finding the perfect balance. He didn't want to rush it. The McKendricks' name held weight in the industry. So much so that a nod from them would guarantee the farm business for years to come. He couldn't make a mistake with their horses; anyone's but theirs. If only he could keep Trip off his back long enough to think without all the doubts clouding his judgment.

Wrapping a towel around his waist, he stepped out of the shower only to hear his cell vibrate against his nightstand again. Sighing, he hit Answer and said, "Give me ten," before hanging up and walking to his closet, throwing on a pair of jeans and a black T-shirt, and shoving on his boots. Shaking out his hair as a means of styling it, he went to work brushing his teeth, curious how the day had just begun and it was already shit. That didn't bode well for his week.

Alex ran a hand over his face as he went through the rest of his morning routine—black coffee, notepad, and pencil. He liked the quiet he felt whenever he jotted down notes. That same quiet never came when he entered things into his phone or iPad. So notepad and pencil for him.

Once out in his three-car garage, he eyed his diesel truck, Vette, and Harley, shaking his head a little that his life required him to walk past three manly vehicles. Instead, he hopped into a small golf cart, but at least he was out of his house. Well, technically Trip's house, but Alex liked to ignore that fact, especially when he was pissed at Trip. And he was heading straight for pissed territory now. It was time he had a conversation with his brother about all the calls—either he trusted him or he didn't. But the thing was, he might say he didn't, and then what?

Alex pushed the thought away and set off down the winding road that led to his, Trip's, and their father's house, then cut left toward the main barn. The sky was dark in places, light in others, the day unsure of its official starting time, like Mother Nature had hit Snooze.

He knew the feeling.

Mama V greeted him as he stopped the cart by her house. Her gray hair was pulled back into a low bun, like always, her face cheery despite the early hour. Mama V's kitchen was forever flowing, breakfast, lunch, and dinner, every day. Supposedly, she'd made Alex and Trip's mother a promise before she died that she would keep the boys fed, and she'd made it her mission to keep the promise.

"How are you this morning, V?" Alex asked as he reached for the protein shake she'd made for him.

"Sky's up, can't complain."

He smiled. "Something tells me my brother wouldn't agree with you."

"Ah, he never really has, and I've never really cared. You might try the same." She winked.

Alex's smile turned into a laugh, and he was thankful he'd stopped there before heading on to the foaling barn. He needed a little kindness before he faced whatever doom lay before him.

Resigned that he couldn't delay any longer, he continued on to the foaling barn, where sure enough, his brother's truck had been parked at an angle—proving that he ran the farm and could park wherever and however the hell he liked. It irritated Alex to no end, but instead of lashing out, he reminded himself that the breeding side of Hamilton Stables could more than triple the earnings of training. Alex might be the youngest Hamilton brother, but if his plan worked, he would bring in the most profit for the family business this year. And then what would they have to say? Nothing, that's what.

"'Bout damn time." Trip walked out of the foaling barn, his Stetson firmly planted on his head, the same cowboy boots he always wore around the farm on his feet. A red-and-black plaid shirt hung loose over his Levis, and though to some he might appear to be an ignorant hick, those in the business knew the truth: Trip was the best trainer in horse racing.

Among owners, Alex felt the weight of his brother's name following him around like a dark shadow that refused to lift. He introduced himself, and immediately owners asked, "Trip's brother, right?" He'd have no choice but to agree, but for Christ's sake, there were three Hamilton brothers, not one, and it was time he and Nick receive the respect they deserved.

Pushing aside his bitter thoughts, he opened his mouth to say that he wasn't late, Trip was early, but then he noticed the two women stand-ing a few yards away from his brother, and suddenly Alex's throat re-fused to work properly.

"Hey, there. Doing okay today?" Emery, Trip's fiancée, asked him as she started over. At five foot nothing and barely over a hundred pounds, she looked like a child beside Trip, but her size fit her job well. She was a rider for Hamilton Stables, and her father was the legendary Hall-of-Fame trainer Beckett Carlisle. Which meant Trip and Emery's relationship owned the title of most unexpected match, but there they were, head over heels in love, wedding date six months away.

But while his eyes were on his future sister-in-law now, she wasn't the woman who'd caught his attention.

His gaze drifted over and refused to lift from the bright redhead beside Emery, her skin as fair as milk except for the occasional freckle. Her eyes were so intensely blue Alex found it difficult to look at her without his mouth falling slack. She wore a simple blue and white cotton dress that hit midthigh, her look so out of place on the farm a normal woman might feel self-conscious, but Alex would bet this woman had never felt self-conscious a day in her life. Why would she? To date, he'd never met a woman who held a candle to her.

"Alex," she said, her voice soft, a hint of modesty there that he'd never understood but cut through him all the same.

He nodded back. "Kate."

Kate Littleton stared at the man she'd had sex with not eighteen months before, curious if he still looked the same underneath his per-fectly fitted T-shirt and jeans.

She tried to remember why she'd ended their dating streak, and then the memory came to her like a spoon full of vinegar. Alex had freaked out when Trip and Emery became serious. Something about complications and awkwardness and other words that really meant freak-out on aisle seven. No really, it meant he had no real feelings for her anyway, which was fine, she was fine. Great, even. But the part that had always gnawed at her was that she didn't want anything from him beyond a chance to spend time with him. Just his time, and was that really so much to ask for?

See, despite the arrogant vibe he put out there, Alex was a gen-uinely sweet and funny guy. She enjoyed being around him, enjoyed his laugh, enjoyed the way the conversation never became stilted. He had a carefree spirit and a sharp mind that could fascinate her with a single comment, then he'd smirk like he knew just what he'd done. But Alex just didn't see himself clearly. Shadowed by his brothers, he'd spent his whole life climbing a hill that only rose higher with each step.

But instead of telling him as much or trying to make him see, she'd said goodbye. She'd rather turn him loose than trust her heart to keep its word to her and remain unaffected.

So one day they sat on his couch watching the Falcons play, both of them screaming at the TV and laughing like old friends, and the next day he was a stranger.

Eighteen months had gone by without a word, which was fine. Completely and totally fine. Kate had things to do. Students to teach. Plays to plan out. Little league games to attend. She didn't need Alex Hamilton, but she *did* want someone. She wanted the movie experience, the soft kisses and walks on the beach and happily-ever-afters.

If only she could find the right man to fill the job.

"We were just heading out," Kate said, suddenly uneasy standing before a man who so clearly *didn't* want the job. "Em?"

Emery's gaze shifted from Kate to Alex and then back, her eyebrows lifting. From the age of twelve, Kate had told Emery every detail of her life. Every detail except those that concerned Alex Hamilton. She could almost hear Emery's brain churning, unspoken question after unspoken question hitting in her mind.

"Caterer tomorrow morning at nine," Emery said to Trip, before rising onto her toes to give him a quick peck on the lips. Only he was having no part of quick and held her to him, giving her the sort of kiss Kate knew would embarrass Emery thoroughly. But instead of her friend reprimanding him as she pulled away, she smiled that smile of someone deeply smitten and said, "I love you."

He kissed her again. "I love you more."

For a second, Kate couldn't decide if she wanted to grin at her best friend's love antics or roll her eyes. It'd make it a lot easier if she had her own guy to kiss and smile at it, but instead all she had was bad date after bad date.

Just last week, she'd accepted Grayson Pierce's offer to go out. He was fine-looking and came from a good family. What could go wrong?

Everything, that's what. From his inability to eat with his mouth closed, two—no three—belches during dinner, and the spaghetti stain on his white golf shirt, Kate would sooner go out by herself than experience another disaster like that.

If only . . .

Her gaze landed on Alex, but then again she'd been there, done that, had the scar on her heart to prove it. Oh well, it was for the best.

The sounds of others arriving at the farm echoed all around them, reminding Kate just how out of place she was there. Emery belonged here, not her. She focused on a small anthill in a patch of grass by the barn and refused to look up, though she ached to see if Alex was watching her. If he remembered their time together fondly or if she'd been another notch on his conquest belt, long since forgotten.

"Alex?" Emery called.

When he didn't answer, Kate looked up, only to find him focused inside the barn, already tuning everything else out.

"Earth to Alex?" Emery repeated.

He turned then, but Kate could tell his thoughts had long since left the threesome and were focused on the mare in the barn, scheduled to foal that day. "Yeah?"

"We wanted to have the wedding party over to Trip's tomorrow for a barbeque. Will you come?"

His eyes drifted almost imperceptibly to Kate, but the impact on her was immediate. How that man could lock her in place with one gaze blew her mind. Trip might be the leader of the Hamilton family, but he didn't have that thoughtful glint in his eyes like Alex. Like his mind worked out complex puzzles the rest of them couldn't even see. It intrigued Kate, and also scared her. A mind like that would never feel content in one place, and it was likely the reason he'd gone from college to college, job to job, unable to sit still, unable to settle down.

Like a wild stallion, his heart would never beat easily unless it was running.

"The wedding party?"

Trip shifted his weight from one foot to the other, clearly uneasy, but Kate didn't want this to get awkward. She was fine. They should be fine, too. This didn't have to get uncomfortable. So she and Alex hung out a few times. They'd been more friends than anything else.

"Yes, come." She bit her lip and forced herself to focus on him.

Alex smirked back at her. "Is that an order, Ms. Littleton?"

She smiled back, enjoying the easiness that slipped into his eyes. "That's right, teacher's orders. Besides, Trip promised to have one of Patty's Bundt cakes there, and I know you can't resist cake."

Their gazes locked.

"No . . . I can't."

Instantly, Kate's thoughts went to the last slice of cake they'd shared, him asking for a bite, a wicked spark in his eyes, and then her lifting her fork to his lips. That perfect mouth of his wrapped around her fork, his eyes on hers, and suddenly the plate clanged onto the floor and he had her in his lap, their hands everywhere, lips connecting, tongues intertwining.

It'd taken a surprisingly small amount of time to undress each other, and even less time to shove the nagging voice in her head to the corner, ordering her to shut her eyes if she didn't want to watch. Because Kate needed that night. She needed it like she needed to breathe. And though a part of her wanted more, she knew that night would be the last one for them.

"So, it's settled. Seven good for everyone? And maybe we should have two cakes," Emery said, her expression thoughtful. "That way we'll have plenty."

Alex turned back for the barn. "Nah, I'll just share some of Kate's." He winked at her, then started for the barn again, when Kate called out.

"Actually, I share my cake with someone else now." The words were out so fast she didn't have time to think about what she'd said or what she'd say next. Which was the real problem with lying—there was never just one. You had to build on the lie, explain and create, and then how would you ever remember all those details the next time you saw the person you'd told them to?

Alex stopped and peered over his shoulder at her. "Is that right?"

No, not even close. But she refused to let him think he could just take a bite from her cake anytime he liked. She crossed her arms and held her head high. "Yes."

He pinned her with that look of his again. The one that made her feel as though she were the only person standing around, the only person in the world. The only person who mattered. And, for a moment, she thought he might regret how they'd left things, might even feel a twinge of jealousy, but instead he said, "Happy to hear it. See you around, *Ms*. Littleton."

Kate stared after him, wishing she could think of something smart to say back, but all she managed was a slight nod before following Emery away from the barn.

When would she learn? If she tested Alex Hamilton, she was the one to get burned.

Chapter Two

"What the hell was that?"

Alex spun around to see his brother leaning against the brown barn door, his head cocked in that way that said he had a thousand opinions and expected Alex to pick up on every one of them.

"What?"

"The cake thing."

Alex knew he should have kept his mouth shut, but somehow when he was around Kate, everyone else melted away and it became just the two of them. Flirty banter took over, and if he wasn't careful, he'd find himself edging closer and closer to her, his body eager to be in her warm space, his fingertips itching to touch her skin.

"It was nothing," Alex said as they walked around to the foaling stall, where Gorgeous Two, a bay mare, walked around and around, Dr. Vickers, the farm's house vet, beside her. Hay covered the floor of the stall, and Dr. Vickers had two of his staff nearby to help. Any second, the mare would lie down and slowly push out the foal, the whole thing beautiful and horrifying. The first time he watched a foaling, he'd thought the mare was going to die. But then the foal stood on wobbly legs and the mare came over to him, the horror from before replaced by the beauty of nature at work.

"Didn't sound like nothing. Sounded like code for—"

"Shh," Alex said, growing frustrated at his brother. Right now wasn't the time to talk about cakes and hidden meanings, and damn was there ever a hidden meaning. A champion mare was delivering her first foal on Hamilton Stables property. This foal could sell for a small fortune, and Alex intended to show the mare the respect she deserved.

Trip took a step toward his brother, his voice as loud as ever. "Did you just *shh* me on my farm?"

Alex turned on his brother and stood tall. "This isn't *your* farm. This is the Hamilton family farm, and guess what? My last name happens to be Hamilton. So I am every bit as much its owner as you. And this?" Alex motioned around him. "This right here? This is my space. I built this foaling barn, had wide stalls put in especially for the mares in foal, and I will not have you agitating my girl when she's potentially producing a multimillion-dollar colt. So either shut up or get out."

For a second, Alex thought his brother might deck him, but instead he cocked his head to the side, like he was seeing his brother for the first time. "All right, then."

"Good."

"I've got a new exercise rider arriving this morning anyway."

Dammit. There went the little bit of respect Alex had earned. "Um . . . about that . . ."

Trip spun around on his heels. "You didn't."

Alex lifted his shoulders, a grimace working its way across his face. "Does it help if I say I didn't know?"

Trip stormed out of the barn. "Outside. Now."

"The mare—"

"Let me fill you in on a little secret. That mare will foal whether you're here or not. Whether Doc Vickers is here or not. Whether the sun is up or the moon. She's an animal, and she knows what the hell she's doing without us interfering. Outside *now*."

Sighing heavily, Alex followed his brother outside. The air had warmed since he'd arrived, spring proving hotter this year than last, and the sky was clear except for the occasional wispy cloud, not a drop of rain in the forecast.

Trip walked down the path beside the barn, around a patch of small trees that had yet to grow large due to too much shade, and then whipped around to face his brother. "I have lost three solid employees over the last year because of your dick."

"Hey, I—"

"And don't think I didn't notice how you were looking at Kate. That's Emery's best friend, her maid of honor. You will not screw around with her."

"I wouldn't."

"You have."

Alex shook his head, before peering up at his brother and sighing in defeat. "Well, I won't again."

"You're right you won't. Or anyone else. I need you to focus. We're poised to become the number one breeder and trainer in the world. We can't jeopardize our credibility right now."

"I know that."

"Do you? Because seems to me you're screwing every female body that crosses your path, without care or regard for how it looks for the family. I need your head in the game here, Alex."

Frustration bubbled up inside him. "It *is* in the game. It's been in the game for over a year now. And I'll prove it."

Trip leaned back on his heels and crossed his arms. "I'm listening."

"I'll go dry for a while."

Trip's eyebrows lifted. "Dry?"

Glancing around, Alex felt like he was eight years old again, chasing after his older brothers, begging them to let him be a part of whatever they were getting into that day. Begging them to see him as more than the little brother. He shouldn't have to do a damn thing to prove to his brother that he was serious, but the truth was, he craved his brother's respect. Trip had taken a chance allowing Alex to take over the breeding arm of Hamilton Stables. He didn't want to let him down.

"No sex."

At that, Trip's mouth twitched. "No sex? Really?"

"What? Since apparently my social life is interfering with work, I'll cut it out."

"You'll cut it out?"

"That's what I said, isn't it?"

"That's what I heard, but you do realize that we're talking about you, right?"

Alex crossed his arms, offended. "I can do it."

Trip walked past his brother, patting his back as he went. "Sure you can, bro. And I'll be happily laughing my noncelibate ass off as I watch you try."

Grinding his jaw, Alex pushed aside his brother's jokes, because at the core of the argument was some truth. Alex needed his head in the game, and he couldn't focus on business like he should if he was dodging women around the farm. Celibacy seemed a steep price to pay for success, but if it helped him gain respect in the conference room every Wednesday, then so be it. Consider it done. Besides, it was only sex. People went without it all the time. He'd be busy at the farm anyway. But then his thoughts drifted back to Kate in that little cotton dress, her skin as smooth as ever, a hint of laughter in her eyes, and he groaned.

Six months until the wedding, which meant six months of barbeques and rehearsals and rehearsal dinners and—

Ah, damn, who was he kidding? This was going to kill him.

By the time he made it back into the barn, Gorgeous Two had foaled a colt, who was already walking around on wobbly legs like he wanted them to lead the way to the track.

"Atta boy," Alex said, grinning wide, a strange feeling working through him. He'd call it pride, but he'd experienced it so rarely it felt unfamiliar. If giving up sex was what it took for him to continue to feel this way and to drive the business to the level where he wanted it to be, then so be it.

Bring it, celibacy.

Chapter Three

Kate adjusted her sunglasses as she approached the stands at Crestler's Key's baseball park, a hint of freshly mown grass in the air. It was a hot day, the sun relentless above, yet still the stands brimmed with people—mostly parents, eager to argue with each other or the umpire or really anyone willing to argue back. She often wondered why old Bill Maxon continued to call the games. Kate had been coming to the park for the last two years, and she'd heard the poor man called every name in the book—sometimes all in the same game. But he never appeared deterred. So to help, Kate had taken it upon herself to bring some refreshments in the hopes of getting the parents distracted enough so the kids could play without their folks embarrassing them.

"Food's here!" she called out to the stands and set down her cooler of mixed beverages and giant bag full of snacks. Like moths to a flame, the parents all started over, and Kate took her spot at the top of the bleachers. If Emery were there with her, she'd roll her eyes and say they didn't deserve the treats, but sometimes you had to offer kindness to the ones who didn't deserve it so the ones who did could receive it, too.

"Hey, Ms. Littleton!"

"Hi, Charlie!" She waved to Charlie Compton at third base, causing him to miss the ball flying from second that would have marked the runner out. Charlie frowned as the second baseman, Mark Saxton, another one of Kate's students, yelled, "Get in the game, Charlie Brown!"

Kate cringed at the nickname, her inner defender eager to scold Mark, but then a small voice from the front row screamed out, "Worry about your own base, Saxton!"

A grin spread across Kate's face as she craned her neck to see Lily Landers standing with her hands on her hips, her white-blond hair held back with a red headband, a simple navy sundress and red flip-flops completing her look. Her gaze drifted to third base, and Kate could almost hear her sighing affectionately in Charlie's direction, but the boy didn't look back at the little girl.

Lily's shoulders slumped and she returned to her seat, her chin resting in her hand as she went back to watching the game. Immediately, Kate thought that third grade was proving more complicated than kindergarten.

She'd taught five-year-olds for three years before deciding she wanted to try something different. And while she still adored the messy faces and forever smiles of her kindergarteners, she loved teaching third grade. She liked the way the kids tried to act like adults but couldn't quite figure it out. Their personalities weren't yet corrupted by *things*, and though she saw more cell phones than she thought appropriate for eight-year-olds, they still had that innocence about them that made her heart happy.

The opposing team got a base hit and the runner on Charlie's base broke for home. Kate rose along with the rest of the crowd as the outfielder threw the ball toward home plate. She watched with pleading hands as the ball soared closer and closer, almost there, almost there. They needed this win like the desert needed rain, but the little runner was too fast and crossed the base a second before the ball arrived in the catcher's glove. Now Crestler's Key was down a run and there was still one out left in this inning.

The next batter stepped up to the plate, and Kate felt a little guilty for silently hoping he'd strike out. She knew that often resulted in slumped shoulders and barely contained tears, but only one team could win this game and it needed to be hers.

He swung at the ball—strike one. Kate prayed harder. Swing, strike two. Then the third pitch came in and *smack*! The ball sailed out to left field and the crowd of parents stood again, but Kate remained seated this time. Greer Grant, another one of her students, played left field, and he was probably the best on the team. She pushed her glasses back into place, reached for her tote bag to grab her phone, and smiled as Umpire Bill signaled the out.

Every single time. The boy had a gift for sure, and she could see the greedy excitement in his daddy's eyes every time Greer played, but Greer also loved to read. Loved to write stories and play pretend. He was athletic, but he was also creative. Kate hated to think that his creativity would be pushed aside in favor of sports. He was a kid after all. Why couldn't he like both? But she learned long ago that what was rational to her wasn't always rational to others.

The next pitch sailed over the plate, and with it, the first argument among parents over whether the pitch was a ball or a strike. And now it was time for Kate to check out. The sports lover in her had too many opinions to sit here quietly while the parents argued over the right call.

She had just decided to pull out some papers to grade when Matt Bridges slipped in beside her. "Is this seat taken?" He had on one of those short-sleeved plaid shirts over cargo shorts, his brown hair styled with gel, and flip-flops on his feet. Which was all fine. The outfit worked and wasn't a problem, but it didn't exactly ooze hot and sexy either. That, coupled with his job as a mailman, and Kate found herself grimacing at the thought of him instead of growing excited. Still, Matt was a good guy, and a few years ago she would have been giddy as a schoolgirl at the thought of him sitting beside her. But now . . .

"This? Here?" She pointed to the spot beside her. "Um, no. Not taken at all." Why did she suddenly sound like one of her eight-year-olds?

"Good game."

Kate turned to him slowly, her eyebrow cocked. "We're down."

Most of the parents were standing now, half of them shouting church obscenities ("Jesus!" "Mother of God!") at Umpire Bill, who, despite appearances, had to be wondering why he'd ever volunteered for this job in the first place.

"Right," Matt said as he pushed his small frame glasses higher onto the bridge of his nose. "To be honest, I'm not really watching it. I came by because I knew you'd be here."

"Oh?" Did Kate sound like she was cringing? Or was that just an internal reaction to the statement?

"Yeah. I came by to ask if you'd like to have dinner tonight."

And there it was, the question she hoped he wouldn't ask, yet why? Why not go out with Matt?

Kate thought of what the teenager Mary Elizabeth, who waited tables at Brighton's Sandwich and Pastries, had said to her once—that she should date a firefighter, not a mailman—and wondered if she was right. Putting aside the fact that Matt assumed she had no plans on a Saturday night, he was indeed a mailman. A good mailman, she assumed, but a mailman all the same. Somehow that uniform didn't conjure the same fantasies as a firefighter. Then again, she'd sampled the firefighter thing and wasn't so impressed.

A loud crack sounded from the field and Kate rose up as she watched Charlie round first to second, and their coach—Mark's father—waving him into third. He ran with all his might, then slid at the same time as the ball soared toward the plate. "Safe!" Everyone in the stands shouted as the umpire fisted his hand, signaling him out, and that was that. The game was over. But then the parents all raced from the stands, Charlie's father at the front, like a commanding officer ready to march his troops into battle.

Kate peered over at Matt, a smile stretching across her face at the chaos brewing on the field. It wouldn't be the first time the sheriff had to come out to one of these games. "How about right now?"

"Sorry, what did you say?"

The screams from the stands had gotten louder, arguments popping up all around them as parents argued whether the game should be over or whether that last out wasn't actually an out at all and the game should continue. The sky had kept its promise to stay blue and light, so as Kate stood and beckoned for Matt to follow, she used it as a sign for her to choose the easy path in front of her. In this moment, that path's name was Matt Bridges. And so what if he was a mailman? Maybe he liked to get kinky in his uniform and mailboxes turned him on and—

No, no, no.

Kate shook her head, else there was no way she'd be able to sit through lunch with him. There was nothing wrong with nice, but a girl needed to feel a certain level of desire for a man, and so far Matt's career choice had done little more than make her curious whether he wore the same tall black socks as her mailman, Harry. Like a standard wardrobe protocol or something. But certainly it wasn't making her insides perk up with interest like a firefighter or a handyman or . . . a racehorse breeder.

Damn Alex for having a hot career, though Kate had an inkling he could be a plumber and she would still find him irresistible. Some men possessed that spark that drew a woman like one of those zombies in *The Walking Dead* to flesh, and it wasn't lost on Kate that

Alex had shown his spark to more than just her in Crestler's Key. In fact, she'd heard his name more than once in conversation at Brighton's, and it made her wonder if those women were discussing him as a fond memory from their pasts or a current experience they were all too eager to sample again.

"Kate?"

"Yes?" she asked, then shook her head because she'd once again drifted into la la land over the youngest Hamilton brother. What was it about those boys that made women stand up and pay such attention? The hair? The deep Southern drawl? The way their jeans hung a little on their hips? She didn't know, but clearly she needed to build up some immunity to it.

"You'd said something back at the stands before the fight broke out." Matt hesitated, like he was afraid he'd heard her wrong and didn't want to embarrass himself. Yet another difference between him and Alex; Alex wouldn't care.

Kate's gaze drifted to the stands to see every person in them standing and sectioned off into tiny groups, all arguing. Over a little league game. She'd told the boys in her class that she would come to their games and she hadn't missed one yet, but she was going to need to bring ear plugs or something if she hoped to survive the rest of the season.

"So?"

Focusing back on Matt, with his gelled hair and glasses, his warm smile that promised easy times, she released a slow sigh. "I asked if now sounded good. To go out?"

That warm smile took over his face. "Now sounds perfect."

He placed his hand on Kate's lower back, which should have created a tingly reaction or giddiness or something, but instead she found herself stepping away from his touch, not ready to go there. She'd crushed on this man for no less than five years and he was asking her out. She should be over the moon with excitement, ready to scream, yet all she felt was disappointment.

"My car's just over there," he said, pointing to the parking lot beside the field.

"Right. Or I could just meet you there?" Kate asked, curious if she would want a way to escape once they arrived, which was just plain ridiculous. Why was she being so shaky with Matt? She'd known him for years now, had crushed on him for most of high school and college. Why did the thought of him touching her, kissing her, make her cringe now? She blamed Mary Elizabeth and her remarks about the fireman-versus-mailman thing. Never had Kate even considered a man's career as a thing. After all, she was an elementary school teacher. That didn't exactly ooze sexiness.

"I can bring you back to your car."

Biting her lip, she nodded and followed him to his Jetta, which really shouldn't have made her cringe still more. She drove a Prius. What right did she have to judge anyone's car? And never once in her life had she even cared about what a man drove. But a Jetta? Really?

Her thoughts drifted to Alex's garage—the Harley, the huge diesel truck, and the vintage Corvette he'd been rebuilding the last time she was there. Maybe he was done now and driving it right this very second. Now those were manly cars, the very definition of sexy, and yet she was sliding into a Jetta.

Lord help her.

"So how do you like teaching third?"

Kate's head turned slowly to the mailman driver beside her. "How did you know I switched to third?"

"I heard Annie-Jean talking about it with Emery at Brighton's last week."

Kate crossed her arms and stared out the window. Why did it suddenly feel like Matt had been snooping on her? And what was wrong if he was? Shouldn't she want him to snoop her? Or sneak her? Or whatever S-word fit the bill? But instead of feeling that sense of excitement she should, the whole thing creeped her the heck out.

"I put in for the change the end of last year."

"Tired of kindergarteners?" He laughed, but a cough hit him at the same time, so the laugh sounded more like a snort. And. Dear. God. Why did she agree to this? And further, why did she have a crush on this man for so many years? Seriously?

Her gaze drifted over to find him watching her. They'd stopped at a traffic light, and he was smiling like a kid on Christmas morning.

"What?" Kate peered around to see what could possibly cause such a smile.

"Nothing. I'm just happy you agreed to the date."

Date? Was that what this was? She thought of lunches as samplings. Nothing serious, no worry of kisses after or roaming tongues. It was all very wham, bam, thank you, ma'am.

"Um, right. Me too."

Matt's expression lit, and Jesus All to the Mary of Heaven and Christ, why did she say that? Thankfully, the light turned and they continued on into town, Matt parking outside AJ&P Bakery.

"We're eating here?"

Suddenly, Matt appeared worried. "Is this okay? I heard they were serving paninis now, and I've been dying to try them. I have no idea why bread pressed together like that can be so good, but I can't get enough of them." Then he turned that bright stare onto the "AJ&P" sign, and Kate almost laughed out loud despite the situation.

Well, if she'd ever hoped for attraction between them, that hope just flew out the car window and straight into AJ&P to have a panini.

Matt came around to open her car door, just as she pushed it open, directly into him. He released a loud *gumpht* and then corrected. "Oh my God, are you all right?" Kate asked, shutting the door.

"Yes. A little bruised maybe, but I'm sure I'll be okay." He patted his stomach again like she'd shot him in the gut instead of opened her car door into him, and the mean girl side of her wanted to tell him that if he hadn't been craning his neck in search of the damn paninis he would have seen the door opening and could have stepped out of the way.

But she wasn't a mean girl.

Mostly.

Matt reached for the door to AJ&P and glanced at her, his eyebrows raised as if to check that there wouldn't be another collision.

"It's just a door," Kate said, opening it and motioning for him to enter. All right maybe she *was* a mean girl. But come on!

As soon as she stepped in after him, her gaze connected with Annie-Jean's, the AJ in AJ&P and Emery's favorite aunt. The smell of freshly baked breads hit her nose and she smiled, memories of her and Emery playing in flour at Annie-Jean's, her ordering them to put that flour to use if they were going to put their hands in it.

"Hey there, sugar," she said, leaning over the counter to give Kate a kiss on the cheek, which left remnants of flour and sugar in its place. Kate wondered if Annie-Jean coated herself in the stuff after her shower every morning, or if it simply stuck to her like an admiring cat to its owner. She wasn't sure, but Kate had never seen Annie without flour on her somewhere.

"Hey, Annie. How are you?"

"Nervous as all hell. I finally agreed to go out with Marty." She leaned in and whispered, "But he's a mailman. What's the likelihood that he'll know how to use his parts?" Kate grinned. Annie had never been one to care about appropriateness. Then Annie's gaze shifted to Matt, already seated at a table close by, and her eyes widened. "You're sampling mailmen, too?"

Kate's flush went straight to her bones. "Apparently."

"Kate, honey, you're too pretty for a mailman. You should date a fireman." Again with the firemen. Then Annie's eyes sparkled and she snapped her fingers, as though she'd figured it all out and could now properly wed Kate off. "I've got it! What about one of Trip's brothers?"

"Yes, what about one of Trip's brothers?" a rough voice said from behind Kate, and she knew without turning who had stepped into their conversation.

Annie held her hands out to Alex. "Exactly. Look at him. Cute as a button, and I bet he knows what to do with his parts."

Dear God, forget my prayer to live to seventy. I'd like to cash in my card right now.

"Indeed I do, Ms. Annie," he said with a wink, flirting with the woman. He had on rugged jeans and a T-shirt, flip-flops on his feet, his hair as messy as ever.

Annie-Jean smiled, because Alex had that effect on a woman. "You are trouble on toast, Alex Hamilton. You know that?"

"It's a tough job, Ms. Annie, but someone's gotta do it." He cocked his head at Kate, that smile of his taking shape. "So are you going to answer Annie's question or are you going to leave a man hanging? Why not get with one of Trip's brothers? I happen to know of one who wouldn't mind splitting his time with you." He looked her up and down, and Kate rolled her eyes.

"Does that crap work on anybody?"

"It works on everybody, and by the look of that flush on your neck, I'd say it's working on you, too."

Immediately, Kate raised her hand to her neck, and if she wasn't bright red before, she sure as heck was now. Her eyes locked on Alex, and the sheer naughtiness in his matching stare made the rest of her burn as hot as her neck.

"Kate?"

At the sound of Matt's voice, she peered over. "Sorry, be right there." Matt's eyebrows drew together as he stared at the menu, and Kate thought he must be deciding between the two paninis AJ&P had on their menu. By the strain on his face, they could be here all day.

"Is that who you're sharing your cake with now, Red, or is he just hoping for a taste?" Alex's gaze flicked over to Matt and then back to Kate. "Can't say I blame the man, but he's not your type."

"Like you know a thing about my type."

"Don't I?"

Before Kate could explain to Mr. Arrogant Hot Guy that just because they'd had mind-blowing sex didn't mean *he* was her type, Justin Prinket walked up to them, his white-blond hair shining bright against his smiling face. His T-shirt claimed he put the *man* in Batman.

"Hey, Ms. Littleton."

"Hi, Justin." She patted his hair, which made him turn as red as Kate had been just moments before. The little boy glanced back to a table in the corner, where, sure enough, Sam and Kyle, two of his friends in class, were seated, both of them laughing at Justin. Crap. She needed to remember that eight-year-olds couldn't be treated like five-year-olds.

Clearing her throat, she tried to start again. "What can I do for you?"

"Well, I was just wondering if you'd chosen Romeo yet?"

Ah, that.

The spring play was months away, but already the students were excited. They'd spent weeks in class planning out the set, working on lines, reading *Romeo and Juliet*, and then watching the movie—until Kate realized it was a little old for eight-year-olds and quickly turned it off.

Now, she smiled at his enthusiasm. "I'll post the list outside my door this week. Then we'll have to get busy building the set." She squeezed his little arm. "Think you're strong enough to help hammer a few nails?"

His eyes widened with excitement. "Yes, ma'am. I have my own tool belt and everything."

"That's perfect. I just need to recruit a few men to help with some of the heavy lifting and we'll get started."

"Great! Thanks, Ms. Littleton. See you Monday."

She started to ruffle his hair again and pulled back, smiling instead. "See you Monday."

As soon as he was gone, Alex stepped in front of her. "Need some muscles, huh? Well, it just so happens I have some. Let me know where and I'm there."

Kate wasn't sure if she should roll her eyes or grin. The man had a way of coming across as adorable instead of arrogant. "Thanks, but this is a Crestler's Key thing. Not sure your Triple Run kin would be so happy that you're offering to help with our spring showcase."

He waved her off, then leaned in close, peering around conspiratorially. "This might come as a surprise, but I don't really care what the town thinks of me."

"Really? 'Cause, see, I think you do. I think that's why you agreed to take over the breeding for Hamilton Stables. I think you want them to respect you, your brothers to respect you. Your father."

All hint of humor dropped from Alex's face, his green eyes burrowing into her like he was trying to figure out a complex puzzle. He shook his head, causing strands of blond and brown to fall across his forehead. But before he could respond, Annie returned from the back of the bakery with three cake boxes. Alex nodded to the cakes, and instead of responding to Kate, he said, "Picking up the Bundt cakes for Emery."

"Ah," Kate said, still watching for a deeper reaction. Then, before she could stop herself, her gaze trailed over the smooth lines of his face, the strong jaw, the defined cheekbones. In another life, he could have been a model, and Kate wondered if he'd ever considered it, with all the careers he'd had in his life before settling into this one. Then again, Alex was far too wild and manly to ever consider such a job. It would be beneath him, she thought.

He grabbed the boxes easily, balancing them one on top of the other in one hand. Emery would have freaked out, and Annie-Jean looked like she wanted to take them back, else he might drop her precious creations. "See you tonight, Red. Always a treat." He winked, then went out the door, as carefree as ever.

"Kate?" Matt asked again, this time nearly pleading. "Are we gonna eat?"

"Right . . ." She watched as Alex got into his truck, and despite his shades, she could tell he was watching her, too. With effort, she pulled away from his magnetic stare and took her seat across from Matt. "What did you decide on?" she asked.

Matt's face scrunched up again. "I was going to see what you chose first. Then maybe I could get one and you the other, so I could try some of both?"

Kate couldn't help but laugh.

Chapter Four

Alex dropped the cakes by Trip's house, then jumped back into his truck to head out to meet his brothers at the cages. They assumed he could never be on time, because all right maybe once upon a time he couldn't be. But he hadn't been a minute late in over a year, and he made no plans to start now.

Parking outside Rock Batting Cages, he started up the slope to find neither Trip nor Nick there yet, which was strange because Nick was always early. Glancing around the parking lot and finding neither of their cars, he took out his cell, and sure enough there was a text from Trip saying he and Nick were at lunch and would be there soon.

He shoved his phone back into his jeans and walked into the shop. Kane Rock sat behind the counter, his arms crossed, his stare focused on the widescreen across from him. A small personal fan rotated back and forth a few feet away from him despite the A/C running in the shop. The once navy carpet of the small shop was discolored in some spots, pulling in others, and coated in mud in others. The faint smell of cigar smoke floated in the air, though Alex had never seen Kane smoke inside the shop.

"Howdy, Kane," Alex said, which resulted in a small nod, but otherwise the old man continued to watch the game. Alex stepped up beside the counter and watched for a bit. The Braves were playing the Nationals. Or, more specifically, losing to the Nationals. Kane scowled at the screen from below the rim of his Braves hat, a Braves T-shirt stretched across his chest, and Alex knew if the old man stood, he'd find him wearing khaki shorts with a small tomahawk embroidered on the cargo pockets. Rumor had it he used to live in Atlanta and was good friends with Skip Caray, the famous Braves broadcaster who'd passed away years ago now.

"Not doing so well, huh?"

Kane didn't respond, and Alex knew he had all of five minutes to lay down his cash and take his tokens before Kane started yelling at the TV, like he was watching a football game instead of baseball. All season long, Kane switched from good mood to bad, depending upon how the Braves were doing, and after their latest trade—which had pissed off every fan they had—Kane's mouth remained in a constant frown.

"All right, then, see you later, Kane."

He grunted again, and Alex closed the door, grinning as soon as he was sure Kane couldn't see him. Until he caught sight of Trip and Nick beside Trip's truck, arguing.

He started over but stopped cold when he heard his name.

"What are y'all talking about? And why are you talking about me without me here?"

"Dad's pushing for you to make a decision on the McKendricks' broodmares."

Alex ground his teeth together. "Explain to me why he came to you two with that instead of me?"

Trip's gaze leveled on Alex and he knew. Because Alex was still the black sheep in Carter Hamilton's eyes. Would he ever step out of the shadow of his past?

"Look, he's just been in a bad mood lately. Not feeling well or something, I don't know," Nick said. "Let's hit some balls, drink some beer, and forget about it for now. We can talk about it later."

"Yeah, later." But Alex knew it would remain on his mind for the rest of the day. He considered calling his father and asking what his deal was, but Trip was the only one to ever call Carter out; certainly never Alex, and Nick wouldn't dare cross their father. But if breeding did what Alex planned on it doing, his father would have no choice but to admit that Alex was as successful, or even more so, than the other two brothers.

Alex set up beside Trip, Nick on the other side of him. He passed each of his brothers a bat and some tokens, then focused on the ball ready to soar toward him from the pitching machine. He hit it square, then readied for the next, his form perfect as he found his zone and held there. This he could do. Sports had always come easily to him, his body adjusting as it needed to with each challenge. He was All-American in baseball in high school, signed on at the University of

Kentucky to play, his sights on the majors, when he felt his focus wavering.

Suddenly, he couldn't remember why he liked baseball, why he started playing in the first place. Then his mother died, his father became downright impossible to deal with, and Alex needed an out.

He spent a year doing nothing but traveling. He'd backpacked through Asia. Explored rain forests in Latin America. Hiked to the center of the Grand Canyon and spent the night with nothing but a sleeping bag and a tiny one-person tent to protect him. He had lived. But at the end of his travels, he'd returned to find that he had seen the world, but his world in Triple Run was unchanged. Trip was still the same headstrong big brother. Nick still walked the straight and narrow. And their father still viewed Alex as the son who shouldn't have happened.

For years, Alex claimed not to care. He worked every odd-end job out there, even exploring bull riding for a solid six months before he realized he could either live or he could be a bull rider. Then he finished his undergrad and sought out vet school, only to quit a year in to go on an excursion in Africa with a woman whose name he could barely remember now.

His dick had led him into more mistakes than any man should ever admit. Which was why he was all too happy to tolerate Trip's taunts about celibacy. For the first time in his life, he was doing something he loved. Something he was good at. And damn if he'd allow sex to screw things up for him.

"I gotta ask." Trip paused on his way to put another token in his machine and eyed Alex.

Alex sighed loudly. "Not you too."

Trip ignored his brother's attitude and pushed on. "Why haven't you made a decision yet? Beastley is the way to go for Lockley. Pedigrees don't lie. He's your match. Choose whoever you want for Tyrant Queen."

Alex continued to swing away. "Maybe."

"Maybe? What the hell does that mean? Who are you considering?"

Gritting his teeth, Alex swung at his last ball, and then spun on his brother. "Is it my call or not? That's what I need to know here. Because last time I checked, my name is above the breeding manager title on our Web site and business cards. So either you trust me to do my job or you do it yourself. You can't have it both ways. I know the science better than you. That's why I'm in this role. Let me do my job."

Trip started to argue before Nick cleared his throat loudly, and both brothers glared over at him.

"For the love of God," Alex said, "say whatever the hell it is you want to say and stop playing the middle man. You've got an opinion. Speak it."

Nick adjusted his footing and held his head high. He might be a nice guy, but he was still a Hamilton, and he wasn't about to let anyone push him around, including his brothers. "I think you're both being assholes. Trip knows racing through and through. He—"

"Yeah, but I—"

Nick tossed up a hand. "You told me to speak, so let me speak."

Alex licked his lips and took a step back to give his ego some room to breathe. Damn if he wouldn't always feel like the little brother who needed to stand taller to be seen, yell louder to be heard. "Fine. Go."

"All right. Trip knows racing." At Alex's expression, he cocked his head as if in warning, and Alex waved for him to go on. "He understands what it takes to make a champion. You, on the other hand, understand the science. You get conformation and the deeper art of breeding. I think you should work together here. Talk it out, listen to each other's opinion, then make the call."

"My call." Alex pointed at himself, and Trip stiffened. He hated giving up even an ounce of control, but Alex couldn't do this halfway. He agreed with Nick that Trip understood racing better than he did, but breeding was different. Sure it involved studying the pedigrees, but it was also going with that deeper gut feeling, and Trip only trusted black and white without peeking over at the gray. Alex lived in the gray.

Finally, Trip shrugged. "All right. Your call."

"For real?"

"That's what I said, isn't it? But know that this foal is already sold. We are breeding for the McKendricks and they expect a champion. We can't deliver anything less or we lose their business on both sides of the farm. Understand?"

"Yes," Alex said.

They stared at each other for another second, then went back to hitting balls. Several minutes passed before Trip went inside and Nick asked, "So what are you going to do?"

"Honestly? I haven't decided yet. But my gut says the answer ain't Beastley."

Alex eyed the main shop, where Trip had disappeared to hit the bathroom. "So what's going on with you lately?"

Nick put another token into his machine and went back to hitting balls. "No clue what you mean."

"You know what I mean. Word at Rudy's is that you stood up two dates in town. You know women talk."

Nick continued to swing, ignoring his brother.

"Seriously? You're not going to answer me?"

"Nothing to talk about."

"This isn't you."

At that, Nick set down his bat and stepped away from the firing balls. "Are you really going to stand there and lecture me on ethical dating? You?"

"We're not talking about me. We're talking about you. And you've yet to have a serious relationship since Brit died. It's time, bro."

"It'll never be time. I might date eventually. But that giant hole in my chest? It's not going anywhere, so why add to it by throwing guilt on top? Besides, I've got other things on my mind."

"Like what?" Trip this time, returning to his spot.

"Yeah, like what?" Alex added.

Both brothers stared at Nick, but he'd been in business far too long to be intimidated so easily. "Stuff. When it's time for you to know, you'll know. For now, I've got it."

Alex studied his brother as he went back to hitting, at the tension in his face, the way he refused to relax. Whatever was weighing on him had to be bad. Hopefully, he'd unload on one of them before it became any worse.

Chapter Five

That night, Kate parked her Prius in the driveway of Trip's house and stepped out, knocking the door shut with her hip as she fidgeted with her purse to drop her keys and cell inside.

She stood up and immediately stumbled, wondering for the hundredth time why she'd bought these damn heels. Two inches she could handle. Three could make her wish she lacked nerve endings in her feet, but she could manage them. Four was just-get-out-of-here crazy. And right now her feet were suffering in four-inch strappy, red patent leather heels that had no right calling themselves shoes because they were not meant for walking. They were meant for standing and looking sexy as hell. And if Alex Hamilton planned to be here and call her Red, then she was going to give him a reason to do it.

She adjusted her white-and-black polka dot dress, the hem grazing midthigh, and tucked her purse under her arm, then started for the door, hoping Emery would sense her pain and offer her a seat. For the rest of the night. But then, if she sat, her dress would slink up and she'd show off her stuff to the whole damn party, and then what? Clearly, Kate made poor decisions, but this one crested the top as one of her worst. Oh, well; at least she would make an entrance.

The door opened after two soft knocks, and there stood Emery, face beaming with a vodka tonic smile.

"Kate!" she called, wrapping her arms around her. "Vanessa's already here, but she doesn't want us to talk about her hair color." Her eyes went wide. "Did I whisper that?"

Kate fought a smile. "No, not even a little bit."

"Damn."

She turned around and shot Vanessa, who was standing by the bar in the kitchen, an apologetic smile. Vanessa was a cousin on Emery's mother's side and had always been a very put-together type of woman. Matching shoes and earrings. Perfect outfit. But today, she'd toyed with what had to be the whitest hair Kate had ever seen.

"It looks great," Kate said, offering her a hug.

Vanessa grimaced. "You're lying."

Pulling back, Kate took in the hair and then her best friend's cousin. "I am. But thankfully, that's what colorists are for—and wine." She reached around Vanessa for a goblet that sat half full on the bar top. "And it just so happens we have one of those here tonight. Drink up."

Vanessa smiled. "You make everything so easy."

"She does, doesn't she?" Emery said, stroking Kate's arm. "That's why I love her. I love you, Kate."

All right, maybe buzzed was a bit of an understatement.

Kate spun around in search of Trip so she could ask him how much Emery'd had to drink, when instead her eyes locked on another Hamilton, this one leaning against the wall across from her, his eyes squinting a bit in that impossibly sexy way. Like they were too cool and carefree to remain open all the way.

Kate mouthed a *hi* to him, and he nodded back, before pushing off the wall and starting for her.

The group seemed to part as he neared, everyone disappearing in opposite directions. Emery walked away to talk to Trip, Vanessa went off to the ladies' room, likely to study her hair a bit more. Poor thing. But there wasn't a woman on the planet who hadn't been there at some point, and any good colorist could fix her right up. Some things were easy like that. And some things were irrevocably messed up, with no hope of a remedy.

Like the one walking toward her right now.

Alex licked his lips as he approached, a pair of low-hanging jeans hugging his hips, a black polo on him, open at the collar, and a smile that spoke of memories and deliciously dirty thoughts. He held a Newcastle loosely between his hands, and his gaze dipped down, tracing the lines of her dress, the curves of her legs, before stopping at her heels and remaining there for what should be an inappropriate amount of time, but on Alex it read like a compliment she'd been dying to hear. His eyes flicked back up to hers. "Well played, Red. Well played."

"Why do you call me Red? It can't just be the hair," Kate said, shaking out her curls. "You've never been the cliché type. Wouldn't want you to start now."

Alex smiled appreciatively, like he hadn't expected her to notice so much about him. Only the truth was, Kate couldn't stop noticing the youngest Hamilton. Something had happened between them that night, and somehow that one encounter had replayed again and again in her mind. She knew he was the last man on the planet she should have a crush on, so she refused to allow herself to go there. But if she would allow it, if she dropped her armor and opened up her heart and mind, Alex would be the man she'd want.

Of course her reasons for walking away then still held today, so she locked up the Alex box and pushed it to the back of her mind. Innocent flirting she could handle, but nothing more. Kate wanted the fairy tale. She wanted a man who shook his head slowly when he saw her because he couldn't believe he'd been lucky enough to land her for a wife. The sweet cuddles in the morning. Screaming passion in the evening. An every day and every month and every year kind of love that lasted until those final breaths at the end of their lives. She refused to settle for less. Even if, deep in her core, she wanted to ignore all those wants just to see if the chemistry between her and Alex could be repeated if they went another round, or if that night had held a bit of magic.

She preferred to think it was the latter, which was easier to dismiss. One night of kisses she'd felt in her toes. One night of slow touches and distant thoughts and orgasms so intense they'd brought her to tears. Surely those sorts of nights weren't a-dime-a-dozen kind of thing. They were rare . . . magical.

In her psychobabble, she hadn't realized Alex had been speaking, so when she heard Matt's name, her head jerked up. Only it wasn't Alex who had mentioned him.

"Sorry, what?"

Emery's eyebrows threaded together. "I asked how the date went with Matt?"

"Oh, that."

"That bad?"

Kate's gaze shifted to Alex, who was biting his lip like it took all the effort in his body to keep from bursting into laughter.

"You got something to say, pretty boy?"

Alex shook his head. "Nah. Nothing." He scratched his jaw, and Kate's eyes were drawn to the fine layer of stubble covering it. She imagined what it would feel like on her cheek if he leaned in to whisper in her ear. If she would hear the soft scruff sound, feel it brush roughly against her and then . . .

Trip called Emery to the backyard, where he was grilling, and Alex's smile lit his face. "You know, if I didn't know any better, I would say you were having less than honorable thoughts right now."

Kate straightened, then reached behind herself to grab one of the glasses of wine Emery had set out. She dropped a few cubes of ice into it that were really meant for the other drinks, but she didn't care. Etiquette be damned. She was never a prim and proper sort of girl anyway.

"You sure have a lot of opinions about me all of a sudden," she said, deflecting his innuendo.

"It's not all of a sudden at all. But I have been curious if—Matt, was it?—got that lunch he seemed so impatient to eat. Or did he go straight for the dessert? Is he a fan of cake, too?"

At that, Kate tilted her glass back, drinking down its full contents, then reached around for a second one. How many did Emery set out? There were only six people there.

"I take that as a no. I told you he wasn't your type."

"Oh really, Mr. Knows-All-Kate-Related-Things? What's my type?" Okay, that glass was hitting her already. Damn her embarrassing excuse for an alcohol tolerance.

Alex took the glass from her hand and set it on the bar beside her. "You should eat before you drink anything else." When Kate opened her mouth to tell him he should worry about himself, not her, he leaned in closer, silencing her with his proximity and the assault on her senses. He smelled like lemongrass and Ivory Soap and man. One hundred percent man. "You want a man who reads to you on the beach. Who knows better than to step in to help when you're struggling with a project. Who gets that you need to figure it out yourself. A man who never opens your car door but always shares his popcorn. Or any food really. A man who's comfortable enough in his own skin to let you brag when your team wins instead of his. A man who makes you want him so badly you never grow tired of him. Even after years and years together, you're still in love."

Kate's heart had stopped in her chest, and she knew if Alex hadn't placed her wineglass on the bar, it would have slipped from her grasp. She stared at him, curious when the feeling had left her fingers and toes and praying Emery wouldn't call them to come out back, because she was pretty sure her legs had turned to jelly and wouldn't cooperate.

She had spent only a few occasions around Alex, yet he understood her better than people who had known her a lifetime. He saw through to the real her. And normally, this would be a sign of something great. A connection. A feeling. Something deeper than casual lust. But that wasn't their story. And what made it so much worse was that she could see him in each of the roles he described. The one reading to her on the beach, refusing to step in to open the jar of jelly when she would eventually get it open herself. The one she could love for years and years.

And then, despite herself, she peered up at him, only to find those vibrant green eyes staring back at her.

"Am I right?"

Once Alex allowed himself to say exactly what he thought of Kate, he couldn't bring himself to look away. He watched her face transform with each spoken word, the hints of embarrassment, the admittance that he was right. And he *was* right. One of Alex's greatest gifts was his ability to read people, a skill he'd inherited from his mother, and within three encounters with Kate, he'd figured her out. She was a romantic to the core, but unabashedly so. She didn't care what others thought of her, and she was prepared to spend the rest of her life searching for what she wanted. Kate would never settle, and that single fact, among others, made him respect the hell out of her.

"I wish you wouldn't say things like that," she said finally, as though she'd just now found her voice again. He liked that he affected her so. She affected him, too.

"Would it help if I said, me too? But I can't seem to speak anything but the truth around you. It's a little jarring." He laughed, and she smiled in return, and God if that wasn't the most beautiful thing he'd seen all day. He thought of the soft sounds she made when he took her to his bed, how she never screamed out, instead saving those noises just for him. Sweet whimpers in his ear, pleas to continue. He'd slept with plenty of women, but none of them had remained in his soul the way Kate had. And now, standing here mere inches away from her, he became sharply aware of two harsh facts.

First, he'd vowed to be celibate, and somehow he didn't think Trip would offer a free pass on his wife-to-be's best friend. And second, he would never be the man Kate wanted and needed. While Alex would love to read to her on the beach, he feared he would grow tired of the book before Kate. Want to set it down, and then what? There was no getting involved with Kate and walking away. And though Alex felt he was more grounded now, his feet firmly planted, that tug in the back of his chest to explore forever taunted him, and he didn't want to leave Kate. Anyone else but her.

Emery called from the back porch then, and Alex took a deliberate step back so he could breathe again.

"Looks like it's dinnertime."

Kate nodded, then took a step and stumbled, her hand going to Alex's forearm for support. The impact was immediate. A shock rocked through him, the sensation so overwhelming and overpowering that when his eyes locked on hers, he couldn't help stepping toward her, his other hand on her shoulder, and dear God he wanted to take her right there. Vows be damned. Brothers be damned. Everything and anything be damned.

"Alex . . ."

He nodded to Kate, as though she'd said what he was thinking. That they needed to separate and fast, before neither would be able to pull away. She was asking him to be the one to do it, to be strong, to do this for her. He cleared his throat and turned away from her, hating himself a little for being so weak, but damn if he'd walk behind her, see those heels she'd worn just for him. He wasn't sure he could contain himself.

"Tell her I'll be right there," Kate said, her words low.

Alex nodded without looking at her and slipped outside the back patio door, allowing the cool night air to hit his face and relax his senses. Trip's patio was a sight to be seen, and Alex made it a point to disappear out back as often as he could when he visited him. The patio itself was all brown and tan flagstone, curving and bending around the backyard landscaping, creating a picturesque look. A fire pit with chairs around it and a fireplace and grill completed the look. The smell of burgers on the grill swarmed his senses, causing his stomach to growl. With everything going on that day, he'd barely eaten.

And he still hadn't made the decision on the McKendricks' brood-mares. He'd tried to force himself to just do it. To sit down, pick up the phone, and make the decision. But every time, doubt had overcome logic and he'd place his phone back in his pocket, unable to choose. If only he had a solid reason to choose Pirate Pete over Beastley.

"You all right?" Nick asked as he walked out after him and sat down beside the fire pit, the fire inside blazing oranges and yellows against the darkness of night.

Alex prayed all evidence to just how not all right he was didn't show on his face. "Yeah, good. You?"

Nick nodded toward the door. "Is something going on with you and Kate? I thought you two ended whatever that was over a year ago."

"Nah, we're just friends. Less, actually." But as Kate stepped through the open doorway, her face flushed from their moment, those loose curls hanging around her shoulders, he wondered if they would ever be nothing to each other. Maybe some people stayed with you forever.

"Nothing, huh?" Nick said. "Come grab a burger before your tongue hits the patio."

Alex shook his head to pull himself from his Kate-infused trance, but the truth was, he liked being around her. She made him feel better about himself, like he was more than a boy among men. Kate was Emery's best friend. Surely Alex could hang around her without wanting her. He could talk to her without basking in that soft floral scent of hers. He could . . .

Who the hell was he kidding? The wedding was in six months and it would take all the self-control in the universe for him to stay away from her.

But then his gaze hit Trip, who was watching him intently, and Alex resigned himself to be good. As boring as good was, it made him a more respectable person in his family's eyes and helped him focus on the prize. For now, he needed to make a decision on the mares so he could notify the McKendricks and get both his father and Trip off his back. Though he suspected no one would sleep easily until the mares foaled and they got to see the horses on the track.

Emery, Vanessa, and Kate set the outdoor patio table and Trip placed the food in the center, beckoning them all to sit. Alex went for the chair farthest from Kate, but Vanessa took that seat instead, and then there was only one chair left open, directly beside Kate. He shot

Nick a look, but he only shrugged in response, then stood, raising his beer high.

"To the happy couple." He smiled over at Trip and Emery. "May you not drive us crazy for the next six months."

"Here, here," Kate said, clinking her water against Nick's beer bottle. "Or you may be standing up there alone that day." Then she winked at Emery. "Kidding." Emery relaxed, and Kate leaned in close to Alex, causing him to stiffen. "Not kidding."

He laughed. "Careful, Red, or you'll be in the doghouse before this thing even gets started. You're the maid of honor. I'm pretty sure that's wedding speak for do-whatever-the-hell-I-tell-you-to-do."

Kate grinned. "See, I plan to keep the wine flowing. If I'm going to be Emery's servant, I plan to get a little humor out of it."

Alex laughed again, and it hit him that he'd never been around a woman who could make him laugh so freely. Maybe they could be friends. That way he could quench his desire to be around her without destroying his vow to remain focused on business.

"So tell me more about the play." He grabbed a toasted bun and set to piling it with a burger, lettuce, tomato, onions, pickles, then another tomato and ketchup and mustard.

His gaze lifted to find Kate watching him with amusement. "How are you going to fit that whole thing in your mouth?"

"Like this." He tilted his head and opened his mouth wide, taking a large bite of his creation, then moaning loudly for full effect, which sent her into fits.

"You're an animal." She reached up and dabbed her finger at the corner of his mouth. "Ketchup." Their eyes connected, the spark between them too strong. Alex's heartbeat kicked up, pounding away like hooves on dirt. He chewed slowly, then swallowed, wishing she would touch him again so he could feel that rush in his blood again.

"Alex, the mustard."

He jerked free from the trance and his eyes locked on Trip, who looked like he wanted to come across the table at his little brother. "Right." Alex passed over the mustard, reading Trip's expression without his brother having to say a word. *Back off. She's good, you're not.*

Clearing his throat, he focused back on his plate. "So, the play?"

Kate picked up her napkin and fanned her face, causing a smile to tug at Alex's lips. "The play? Oh, right. It's *Romeo and Juliet* with my third graders. I can't believe how excited they are. We're building a full set at the school, hoping to use it every spring for a spring showcase. Maybe even sell tickets to the parents to raise money for the school."

Alex nodded as he took another two bites. "Sounds good. When do you need me there?"

Her hand stopped in midmotion, a forkful of potato salad hovering there like she'd forgotten what she was supposed to do with it. "What do you mean?"

"I was serious before. I'd like to help."

Kate's gaze went immediately to Emery, who nodded encouragingly, but Alex could see his brother had a completely different opinion about this. What? He couldn't help kids now?

"All right. Saturdays at three for the next month. I'm packing snacks for the kids. I'll bring you something, too."

His eyes lit. "What about cake?" He couldn't help it.

"No cake." She shook her head but smiled, and though Alex knew this walked that line he wasn't supposed to cross, he was excited to spend more time with her. Plus, they'd be surrounded by eight-year-olds. How much trouble could he get into?

Chapter Six

Kate pulled into Trip's driveway to pick up Emery the next day. They were scheduled to try on dresses at Always Bridal, a boutique in Lexington. Emery had been looking through bridal magazines for weeks when finally she'd stumbled upon the perfect dress. The cut, the details, everything she wanted, and by some miracle they had it at Always Bridal. Otherwise, this little adventure would take them to Atlanta instead of Lexington.

"Sorry. I was on the phone with Mama," Emery said as she climbed into the Prius.

"Is she still mad that she's not coming?"

"I won't be shocked if she shows up there anyway."

Kate continued out of Hamilton Stables and onto the main road. For months now, Emery had stayed with Trip every night, and by now, she likely had more things there than at her own place.

"Tell me again why you don't want her to go?"

Emery shrugged. "She has a very clear vision of what she wants me to wear. Her only daughter and all. I'm afraid she'll hate everything I like and I won't get something I love because I'm afraid of disappointing her."

"She's your mother, though, Em. She has to see you in your dress."

"She will. But is it such a bad thing to let her see me in it once I've chosen? Besides, she has a hair appointment today, so she wanted me to move our dress appointment to this afternoon, and you have your first play practice to build the set."

Kate knew Emery was convincing herself as much as anyone, and this was her wedding after all, so she let it go. "Fine. But the next appointment she's there, and even if you find it today, maybe we should tell her you didn't, so she can feel like she's seeing you in it for the first time."

"Good thinking."

Emery tucked her feet into the seat and reached for her water bottle. "So, are you going to tell me what was up with you and Alex at the house last night? And what happened with Matt?"

"I just can't seem to go back with Matt. I think I'm different now, maybe, or maybe now that I've been with Alex, nothing else feels right."

Emery stared at her. "Nothing else? You really like him, don't you?"

"He makes me laugh and think. And forget controlling my feelings. They're out of control around him. It's intense."

She nodded. "And you're not worried he'll hurt you?"

Kate thought about the question. Was she worried? She knew she should be, should be cautious and hold him at a distance. "We're not really anything to worry about."

"It didn't seem like nothing last night."

Yeah, Kate thought, *it didn't feel like nothing either.*

It felt amazing and real, the first time she'd longed to see a man in what felt like forever. And then, the moment their eyes connected, she didn't want to let go. If he'd asked her, she would have talked to him all night, listened as he discussed breeding and horse racing and anything else, so long as she could hear that passion in his voice. But maybe what she enjoyed as much about him was how he listened to her with the same intensity. He never interrupted or acted as though he were waiting for his chance to speak. No, he listened, really listened.

"Well, I want you to do whatever you want to do. But I don't fully trust the guy, so just promise to be careful."

"He's your brother-in-law."

"Not yet. But yeah, he will be. And I'll treat him like family, but he's also been with most of the women in both Crestler's Key and Triple Run. He's had a ton of different careers and changed his major like six times, Trip said. It just speaks of someone who can't settle, or refuses to. You want the movie ending. I don't want you to have anything less."

"I won't."

"Kate . . ."

"I won't."

They arrived at Always Bridal with a bit of tension between them, though Kate tried to shake it off. Emery was just trying to protect her, but she was a grown woman, and so what if she wanted to hang around Alex? That didn't mean she wanted to marry him. He might not be her forever guy, which was fine. Completely fine. But that didn't mean she couldn't enjoy spending time with him now.

Of course he might not want to spend time with her, which would make it a moot point.

They slipped into the shop, a bell dinging as they went, and suddenly they were surrounded by a thousand wedding dresses, some matte, some shiny. Some strapless, some sleeved. Some long, some short. It was overwhelming.

But when Kate turned and saw the smile on Emery's face, she couldn't help smiling back. "Let's find your dress."

The store smelled decidedly of spiced potpourri and alcohol. Kate wondered if they sanitized the dresses after each girl tried them on or something, and then sprayed air freshener to try to cover it up.

"Where do we start?" Emery asked, and of course a sales associate with far too much hairspray in her black bob and far too perfectly manicured nails walked up, one hand out like she'd been showing these dresses her whole life. She wore a tailored navy suit and a pink blouse underneath, setting off the shade of her lipstick. Kate could tell Emery wanted someone else to help her the moment this one spoke.

"Ladies, thank you for joining us today. I'd love to introduce you to your perfect dress. Do you have something in mind?" She gripped Emery's shoulders and spun her around, scrutinizing each part of her body, until finally Emery backed out of her grasp, clearly uncomfortable. Enter Kate's role.

"Thank you, but we were just looking for today."

The associate's smile tightened. "Of course. When's the big day?"

"August," Emery answered, and the woman's eyes went wide.

"And you haven't chosen your dress yet?"

"No," Kate said. "She hasn't. But that's why we're here, so if we could just . . ." She motioned to the racks of dresses at the farthest corner from where they stood, and the woman finally relented. "Of course. Let me know if you need anything at all."

Emery draped an arm around Kate in thanks, and then it was all business. They walked around from rack to rack, sliding out dresses and shaking their heads, laughing at the gaudy ones and ogling the beautiful ones, and then, finally, Emery had four picked out, and she disappeared into the fitting room. Kate sat down in one of the chairs before the large three-way mirror, fixed around a pedestal, and she couldn't help wondering if she would ever stand up there, smiling at her mom and Emery, her eyes glistening as she took in her appearance.

And then, as though fate wanted to laugh at her, her phone vibrated in her purse. She pulled it out and peered down to find a text from Alex, Mr. Flirt-But-I-Don't-Really-Want-You.

What time to help with the set?

She tapped the phone against her thigh, her gaze drifting to the mirror, her reflection shining back at her. Like it wanted to remind her what a terrible decision this was, allowing him to step into the safe parts of her life.

"What about you?" the associate asked as she returned from helping Emery into a dress. "Do you need to look at bridesmaid's dresses, or maybe your own wedding dress?" She beamed at Kate until her stare went to Kate's ringless left hand, and then she appeared embarrassed.

"No, no wedding dresses for me, thanks. But yes, I'm sure we'll look at bridesmaid's dresses later. Thanks."

Kate focused back on her phone in hopes that the associate would go away and not stand there while Emery came out. She felt sure Emery wouldn't confess her true feelings about the dress with the lady standing there, potentially offended.

"Well, if you don't need anything else?"

"We're fine," Kate said, smiling too brightly back. "But we'll be sure to call if we need help again. Thanks."

She walked away and Kate released a breath, then eyed her phone again. Logic be damned; she wanted to see Alex. Wanted to laugh at his jokes and enjoy that smile of his. Before she chickened out or Emery emerged, chastising her for having thoughts about Alex again, she typed back **three o'clock**, then dropped her phone back in her bag, but immediately she heard her phone buzz again, and she couldn't help it. She had to know if it was him.

Pulling it out quickly before Emery came out, she glanced down and smiled.

I'll be there, tool belt on and properly stocked.

"What are you smiling at?"

Kate jerked back, startled, but her shock quickly turned to joy as she took in Emery on the pedestal. "Oh my God."

"I know right?" Emery said, swishing a bit and frowning at her reflection. "It's like they had a poof quota to fill or something. It's horrible." Then she glanced around quickly and ducked down, searching, Kate knew, for the annoying sales lady.

"I sent her away."

"Thank God." Then she turned and faced Kate. "What do you think? Seriously. Terrible?"

Kate shook her head, her gaze sweeping from the strapless bodice to the intricate stitching down the dress's full skirt. "It's gorgeous." Then her gaze lifted back to her friend. "I can't believe you're getting married."

"I know. It's crazy and amazing and crazy again for good measure. But I'm so happy."

Kate stepped up on the pedestal and hugged her longtime friend. "I'm so happy for you."

"I want you to have this, too," Emery said, pulling away to look at her friend. "This is your thing."

Kate ran a hand down the dress, fluffing the train and standing back to look at it. "Yeah, but it's not my time now. It's yours. Enjoy it. I'll have my time."

She hoped.

Alex pushed through the door of Triple Run Diner, eager to steal a table in the back corner and get lost in his binder, pouring over pedigrees and stats and on and on until the decision came to him. Every day he opened his binder, flipped through the seventeen tabs, each for a different horse or category or theory, only to close it again at the end of the day, no more sure of what to do than he'd been when he'd opened it that morning.

"Must be something going around the farm," Becca, the diner's favorite waitress and a longtime friend of the Hamilton family, said.

"What do you mean?"

But then he followed her gaze to the booth in the back corner and realized what she meant.

"Must be. I'll join him."

"Your usual?" she asked.

"Actually, if you could bring me coffee and keep it coming that'd be great."

She nodded. "Sure thing, honey." Then she disappeared behind the counter, and Alex focused on the back booth, on Nick's form hunched over a mess of paperwork on the table. He wondered what was going on with his brother, and why he didn't feel he could talk to Alex or Trip about it.

"Becca says you're scaring the rest of her customers," Alex said, sliding in across from him. Nick jerked up, his eyes on Alex, then the papers, and in one swoosh, he piled them up and stuffed them into his briefcase, then closed it, his fingers opening and closing the lock twice, as though he wanted to make sure it wouldn't pop back open so Alex could see everything he was trying so hard to hide.

"What was that?" Alex asked, not willing to give his brother the out he so obviously wanted.

"What?"

"Those papers you just hid like they held all the government's top secrets."

"Nothing." Nick turned, his eyes shifting around, looking for someone, and Alex knew exactly who he sought.

"She went into the back."

"Who?" Nick asked, but he didn't stop his perusal of the diner.

"You know who."

Nick's gaze flipped to Alex, no hint of humor in his eyes. "Actually, I don't. And if you have something you want to say, then say it."

Alex leaned in. "I have a lot of things I want to say, but you've been so shady lately, I don't know where to start. Like should I start with whatever you're hiding from Trip and me? Or the fact that you refuse to publicly go out with a woman? Or the fact that you've had your eye on Becca for more years than I could count, but you refuse to do anything about it?"

"What? I don't have my eye on Becca."

Alex nodded. "Sure you don't. Which is why you're not watching that door for her to come back into the diner right now."

Nick's head snapped back around. "She's a friend."

"Right. A friend."

"What the hell's your problem?"

"Lots of things these days, but in this moment, you. I want to know what you're hiding from us."

"I already told you," Nick said. "I'm not hiding anything."

Becca appeared then, her eyes darting between the two brothers, both of them tense with anger. "Should I come back?"

"Yes."

"No."

"Well, because that was crystal clear, I'll give you another minute." Becca turned, and Nick's eyes locked onto her as she went, a hint of pain crossing his face before he smoothed his expression again and he peered back at Alex like he'd been running a marathon for days and months and years and no longer had the strength to continue. "What do you want me to say?"

"The truth."

Nick's gaze lifted to his brother's. "I can't do that."

"You can't or won't?"

Nick drew a breath. "Both."

Becca returned again with Alex's coffee, and Nick took the out. He collected his briefcase in a hurry. "Meeting in an hour."

"Right." Alex watched his brother rush out of the diner, and Becca peered down at him.

"What was that about?"

"No idea, but I plan to find out." He checked his watch and cursed. "Sorry, but can I take this to go? I forgot I have somewhere I have to be."

Alex thought of Kate directing her students, and before he could stop himself, a smile spread across his face.

"Looks like something good," Becca said, passing him his check.

"No," Alex said, handing back enough cash to cover the coffee and tip. "Something great."

Chapter Seven

K ate walked through the heavy double doors of Key Elementary's auditorium that afternoon, curious whether they'd renovated the place since it was built some thirty years before. The same burgundy-cushioned chairs filled the audience, more than a few of them with stains or fading or holes. The stage itself was all a mahogany wood, with telltale scrapes and marks from years of performances and awards shows. The auditorium smelled of putrid chemicals and dust and years of people before her. All of them in these seats, watching their little kids walk across the stage at one of the awards shows. She wondered if she would ever see her own children walk across the stage.

For now, her focus was on her class of eight-year-olds and their excitement over the first set-building session. Kate had planned three weekends to build the set, and then three to practice the play, plus a few rehearsals during the week just to be safe. Today, she'd had wood delivered to kick-start the process, but as she peered around the auditorium she found only a few sheets of plywood laid out haphazardly and then one stack of two-by-fours. Her students, and their overly critical parents, would be by any second to work on the set, and all Kate had was a few piles of wood?

She surveyed the pile closest to her, wondering if maybe it just looked like a small amount of wood and really this could all build a house or something. But it didn't look like it was enough to build a house, or even a doghouse for that matter.

Hands on her hips, she peered around for someone she could yell at about this but came up empty, so she took out the set design she'd pulled off the Internet the night before. If she sketched out the look, the kids could paint it, which might turn out crazy, but at least it would be fun, and Kate had learned long ago that if she made things fun the kids would come back again and again.

Resigning herself that she'd have to move the wood around and organize it herself, she bent down to grab a sheet and immediately stumbled as her too-short arms tried to steady it without toppling over.

"Woah there, cowboy," a deep voice called from the side door, and Kate peered over to find Alex watching her with a comical expression on his face.

"What are you grinning at?" she asked.

"You realize that piece of wood is bigger than you right? Or are you one of those women who genuinely refuses to ask for help?"

Kate huffed. "You know I am. Now get over here and help anyway."

He took the plywood from her. "Where do you want it, boss?" His eyes crinkled in amusement, and Kate thought she must have been really, really drunk to agree to him coming here.

"Take it to the stage. They laid down some brown paper to protect it, so we can paint."

Alex's eyebrows lifted. "You realize that won't work right? They're kids."

Her gaze drifted to the brown paper, the paint, then the stage. "You're right."

"What was that?" He cuffed a hand around his ear. "I didn't quite hear you. Can you repeat that?"

Kate huffed and went past him, grabbing the cans of paint and brushes. "I said follow me outside, and if you speak another word about it, I'll give them the green light to paint you instead of this wood."

He grinned again. "My lips are sealed. I'll be a good boy from now on."

"Somehow I doubt that."

They stepped outside and into the warm air, and Kate worried that it might get too hot to have the kids out here for long. It was April, so not the ninety-plus degrees of summer, but it could be every bit of eighty degrees. She'd have to think of something fun to cool them off. But it was a perfect day, with a perfectly blue sky, and the sun was out to play, her rays shining down on them, ready to make them sweat.

Reaching down to touch the grass in a field nearby, she nodded for Alex to bring the plywood over and set it down. "It's dry."

"All right, and how will the principal feel about you getting paint all over the field?"

"Field Day's next week. It'll get destroyed anyway. We'll just call it an accident."

Alex propped open the auditorium door and went back in for another sheet of plywood, this time returning with four, his biceps bulging from the stress of carrying them. Kate took the opportunity to take him in. Tan cargo shorts with worn fringe here and there at the ends. Fitted white T-shirt with the green Hamilton Stables logo printed across his broad chest. His dirty blond hair was pushed off his forehead, but she knew as the day carried on, it would inevitably end in a mess on his head. A fine layer of stubble covered his jaw, and she wondered if he purposely shaved so he always had that slightly rugged look or if he let it go and shaved only when he must.

"Are you staring at me, Ms. Littleton?"

Jerking back, Kate dropped her gaze to the paint cans and pretended to organize them by color. "Of course not."

"All right, I'll give you a hundred dollars right now if you can tell me what I'm wearing." He turned her around and placed a hand over her eyes. Without thinking, she drew a breath, taking in his spicy, lemony scent, and before she could order her mouth to be good, she released an audible sigh.

Alex chuckled, his chest rumbling against her back, and it was then she realized how close they were to each other. "Hundred bucks your way, Red. Just tell me what I'm wearing."

Gritting her teeth, Kate tightened her spine. "This is stupid."

"Just admit you were checking me out and you get your hundred. That has to be the easiest payout on the planet."

The smile in his voice was enough to make her consider stomping on his foot and rushing away with her arms crossed, like one of her students, if she didn't get her way. But while Kate liked to consider herself a responsible adult, she could use a hundred dollars. Hell, who couldn't? Right—the Hamiltons. That's who.

But her pride wouldn't allow her to admit to the man she couldn't have that she'd not only been checking him out but had filed away in her mind everything he'd ever worn every time she'd ever seen him. It was less to do with Alex and more to do with the way her mind processed things around her. Though even that was an excuse. She liked to categorize things, true, but this was also Alex. She liked how carefree he was with his wardrobe, yet every time she saw him he looked put together in his own non-put-together way. It fascinated her how a person could be so appealing with so little effort.

"Admit it, Red."

"I have no idea what you're wearing."

Alex leaned in close to her ear. "All right, fine. Be stubborn. How about I tell you what you're wearing?" He turned her around, then closed his eyes.

"Jeans shorts. Yellow tank top. Gold flip-flops with little sparkly things on them."

"How . . . ? " Kate cleared her throat. "Lucky guess."

Alex opened his eyes and peered down, a smile stretching across his face that said *I'm right. Always.* "No such thing as luck. Smart people pay attention."

Her eyes lifted to his. Every time she thought Alex was a carefree guy with nothing but one-liners, he said something like that, reminding her that below the façade was an intelligent, driven man who would do anything to reach his goals.

She wondered what might have happened between them if they'd met five years from now, when he had the breeding business established. Would they have gotten serious after that one eventful night of cake or would they still end up here as friends? Or maybe they weren't friends. The thought made her sad. As much as she enjoyed flirting with Alex, she also liked him. Not liked him, liked him—though a bit of that, too—but mainly just enjoyed his company. How he refused to be anything but real. He said exactly what was on his mind without a hint of embarrassment or worry over how he would come across. To Alex, there was only honesty and the truth. No beating around the bush. But then, being as hot as he was gave a person the ability to speak freely without worry of consequence. Pretty people got away with saying things that others would receive glares for saying—people with freckled skin and wild curly hair. Like her.

But then, Kate had lost her ability to care what people thought around ninth grade, when she still had the freckles and wild hair but also a mouth full of braces and an extra ten—okay, twenty—pounds to her small frame. She worked hard to keep herself in nice shape, but she'd decided long ago that she either lived for herself or she lived for everyone else. Most of them weren't worth worrying about anyway. So Kate shaded her eyes from the sun and peered up at Alex. "I like having you around."

A warm smile touched his lips, all genuineness and pure happiness. It was the polar opposite from the smirks and grins he usually flashed around like a camera gone berserk. This smile was sweet, and Kate found herself wishing she could hold on to it a little longer. "I like being around."

Their eyes locked again, and Kate couldn't help allowing her gaze to drop to his lips, full and ready to be kissed. God, she'd loved kissing him. It had been eighteen months and the memory still sent a chill from her spine to her toes. But she stared a little too long, and Alex cleared his throat, stepping back. "So where do you want me?"

Kate broke from looking at Alex's lips, immediately feeling her cheeks burn, though she felt sure it was less to do with embarrassment and more to do with the other thoughts swarming around in her head. "The kids will be here in less than an hour, and I wanted to have the wood sketched out so they could paint. Then we can get to using hammers and nails, which scares me a little, but I promised all of them I'd let them hammer at least one nail." She cringed at the image of one of them crushing his fingers and an ER visit. Oh well, live or don't, crap happens.

"I didn't realize you did the art thing. I thought you were a sports fan through and through?" He nodded to the Titans hat as she slipped it on to help shade her face from the sun.

"That's such a man thing to say. A woman knows better."

"What does that even mean?" Alex said, the warm smile from before replaced by his hot-guy grin.

"You can scream as your team scores in the last seconds of a game and still appreciate going to the Met. Besides, you like sports and art."

He stared at her, prompting her to continue.

"The breeding thing. You once said it's more art than science, a feeling and analysis of pedigrees and stats and all the things that makes no sense to me, and then you still go with your gut."

"Gut, yes. But you never ignore the science. Every registered Thoroughbred can be traced back to one of a handful of lineages.

That sort of science and detail and effort to maintain stud books can't be ignored. It deserves proper attention." He worked his bottom lip between his teeth, clearly in deep thought, then his gaze met Kate's. "What?"

"Nothing. Just . . . I like to hear you talk about it. Breeding. It fascinates you. Your face completely changes."

"You should come by the barn sometime. Let me introduce you to the horses."

Kate felt an unnatural warmth spread through her at the invitation, which was stupid. And silly. And stupid again for good measure. Still, she smiled all the same and said, "Sure. Name the date."

Just then the sound of a car pulling up jerked Kate's attention from the man before her, but as she took in the Jetta and the driver behind the Jetta's wheel, she found herself wishing she could be as straightforward as Alex. Maybe then Matt wouldn't be walking toward them right now. She never should have agreed to that lunch, and since, he'd called her no less than five times. Damn Emery for giving him her number last year. Now she was going to have to change her phone number and move out of Crestler's Key. Or have the conversation she hated having.

"You didn't tell me you invited the new cake eater."

Kate shot Alex a look that could make a perfectly happy baby burst into tears, then flashed Matt a smile, then, thinking better of it, relaxed her face and put her hands on her hips.

"Matt. Hey. What are you doing here?" Today he had on a *Harry Potter* T-shirt that read *Ravenclaw for Life*, which irked Kate more than it should. Who cared if he wanted to be a Ravenclaw? People could be whatever they wanted to be, like how she would be in Gryffindor.

Matt took in Alex, standing there in that relaxed stance of his, one arm draped over a sheet of plywood like he could lift it up with his pinky if he wanted. And come to think of it, Kate wouldn't mind seeing him try, just to see those muscles flex and—*Stop it!* She thought, stomping once for good measure, which drew confused and concerned looks from the two men. Then it occurred to her that she mustn't have simply thought the words but instead screamed them out, which was awesome. As though this weren't awkward enough, now they both thought she had a few screws loose. And clearly she did, because exhibit a) Alex and exhibit b) Matt.

"Are you okay?" Matt asked, but it was Alex who answered.

He popped her once on the back gently and grinned up at Matt. "She's right as rain, just comparing desserts."

Matt's eyebrows threaded together, and Kate thought she might ask them both to leave, else she end up embarrassing herself to the point of no return. Forget leaving Crestler's Key; she'd have to leave Kentucky.

But instead of vocalizing any of that, she ignored Alex and said, "Yep. Fine. I'm just going to go over here and sketch out the set. If you could help bring around the rest of the wood that would be great."

Matt glanced over at Alex again; then, the forever good guy, he held out his hand. "Matt Bridges."

Alex flashed him that cocky grin of his. "Alex Hamilton."

"Hamilton? As in . . ." Matt took in Alex's T-shirt, the green Hamilton Stables logo in the center, and backed up as though he no longer knew how to act around Alex. It wasn't an uncommon reaction around the Hamiltons, and Kate felt bad for half a second.

The Hamilton family had money coming out of their ears, then more tucked in their pockets for good measure. It was unsettling, and though the Carlisles were wealthy, too, it was an entirely different kind of wealth. The Hamiltons were businesspeople first, owning companies and land and God knew what else, long before Trip settled into training. They'd had the farm, but as far as Kate knew, it wasn't a productive farm by any stretch of the imagination until Trip had stepped in and grew it to the major business it was today. Which explained why he was so hard on Alex. He'd built Hamilton Stables from the ground up. She thought of her third graders working on their landscape dioramas earlier in the year, and how devastated one of them would be if something happened to any piece of the project.

Trip treated the farm like his own personal baby, and though she respected him for putting such care into it, she thought it was time he trusted Alex. Saw him for the intelligent businessman he was behind all that sexy smirk and hair and body.

"Yep," Alex said, as careless as ever.

The two men stared each other down before, thankfully, a group of parents showed up and started toward them. Great, now the parents were here, and Kate hadn't sketched out the plans yet. Well, she remembered that two of her students were fairly artsy and the rest could work with Matt and Alex.

"Here," she said, passing a printout to each of them. "I'm going to work on the sketch. You two handle this."

A smile touched her lips as she took in their expressions, Alex scratching his head as she walked away. "I didn't sign up for this now."

She grinned over her shoulder at him. "Sure you did. I brought a few extra hammers if you need them. They're in that paisley Thirty-One bag over there."

"Thirty-one? What the he—"

"Nah ah ah. Language. You're among God's children now."

Alex licked his lip. "I thought we were all God's children."

"With some I'd say that's debatable." Then she winked at him and stretched out the plans for the tower she'd chosen and went to work sketching it out. The heat of someone's stare bore into her back, warming her insides, until she realized it could be from Alex or Matt, and she didn't want to chance it being the latter enough to turn to see for herself.

So instead, Kate called over two of her third graders and went to work on the sketch, a thrill of excitement working through her despite her brain telling her to be more sensible.

Where Alex was concerned, she was a fool, but damn if it wasn't fun being foolish.

Chapter Eight

Alex walked into the clubhouse of Hamilton Stables, on his way to meet with Dr. Vickers to discuss the matches for the McKendricks' prize broodmares. He thought of his conversation with Kate the day before, how a match was more art than science and how he'd defended the science. And he would defend it all over again if they had the same conversation today, but that didn't change the fact that it was more complex than the way it appeared on paper. Would a stallion with stamina match well to a broodmare with speed? Maybe. Maybe not. It helped of course if a stud had successful offspring. If he proved to produce champions. And while they had Beastley, who'd produced three champions, most of the other four studs they kept at Hamilton Stables weren't as established. Alex went with his gut with each of them, and they hadn't been doing this long enough to know if he was right.

But the McKendricks wouldn't accept anything less than a perfect match. They boarded their best broodmares at Hamilton Stables with the intention that Alex would breed them with the right stud, handle weaning the foal; then Trip would take over and train them a champion. This deal had the potential to set up Hamilton Stables for a very, very long time, and he couldn't wreck it.

Alex walked through the wide main front doors, all wood and stained a deep reddish-brown, almost like a chestnut's coat. Waving to Nancy, the admin, he continued on down the long hallway of offices for the various divisions it took to run Hamilton Stables—marketing, support, events, tours—until he passed his father's office. He started for the doorknob, intending to peek his head in to say hello, when he caught a heated conversation coming from inside.

"You have to tell them."

Alex stilled at Nick's voice, sure he knew exactly who *them* was. The conversation back at the diner ran through his mind, Nick's intensity, and him rushing to hide all those papers. But never once had he considered the secret could involve their father.

"I'll tell them when the timing's right."

"You're running out of time," Nick said, his voice softened now. Tortured. "Why can't you see that?"

Alex's heart stopped. Running out of time? For what? But before he could listen for more details, the office beside his father's opened. He pulled away reluctantly, his eyes on the door for a second longer, before he continued on down to Dr. Vickers. Whatever had Nick so upset had to be serious, but Alex couldn't tell if the issue was with his father or some part of the business. Surely if it were health related they would have told him and Trip. So it had to be work, but what?

Finally, he arrived at Dr. Vickers's office and knocked once before walking on in. One worry at a time.

The old man stood by the window, peering out at the expanse of grassy fields behind the clubhouse. A few mares and their foals were out grazing in the pasture. Dr. Vickers had been the farm vet for most of Alex's life, which meant more times than not he agreed with whatever Trip and Carter said. There was a reason they kept him on the payroll.

"You're early."

Alex grinned. He was getting that a lot these days . "Got tired of missing the first five minutes of everything. Started trying the early thing."

"How's that working for you?" Vickers asked, turning to grin at him. Like always, he wore a Hamilton Stables embroidered button-down and khakis. The same outfit he'd worn every day since Alex was little.

"About the same, honestly, but I'm sure in time things will change."

Dr. Vickers stared at Alex, likely sensing his deeper meaning. For now, Alex could do everything right and he would still be the black sheep. But things were going to change for him. With his family and with his future.

He thought of Kate working so hard yesterday with the kids, and him trying desperately to keep busy, else he'd find himself watching her, mesmerized by that glow that radiated off her, the smile that never left. She wasn't just good at her job. She was born for it, and as the day continued, he found himself picturing her beside him one day, hand in hand as she called after their children. The thought both scared the shit out of him and made him feel oddly at peace. But he wasn't ready for an I-do or even a commitment. He had to focus on business if he hoped to prove himself.

If only he could ask Kate to wait; but then, he couldn't guarantee he would be worth the wait. Though Alex hated that his family didn't trust him, a part of him couldn't blame them. He'd failed at everything he'd ever tried.

Alex took a seat in one of the chairs in front of Dr. Vickers's desk, which was piled with organized stacks of paper here and there, each six inches thick. Who could guess what information lay within each sheet? "How long before you need to go on rounds?"

The man ran a hand over his salt-and-pepper beard, which matched his hair perfectly. "Thirty minutes."

"We'd better get started, then."

Setting down his notebook, Alex flipped to the third tab and peered down at his notes.

"You realize my opinion is the same as it was last week right? Beastley is your stud for Lockley. His stamina will match with her speed perfectly. Both were champions."

Alex lifted his gaze to the man. "Beastley only won three races ever. Sure, one was the Breeders' Cup. But I'm not sure three races makes him a champion."

"It's more than that. He's produced champions."

At that, Alex stood up and walked over to the floor-to-ceiling window, the curtains pulled back to let in light, the blinds raised high and likely never lowered. "He's produced a few champions, but no great races. Again, is that really what we consider a champion?"

Vickers set down his glasses and rubbed his eyes with his forefinger and thumb. "You want Pirate Pete."

"He's the best choice for Tyrant Queen. He won the Derby. She won the Oaks."

"Yeah, he did, but you're matching speed for speed without any history of stamina, and you know you need both."

Alex rested his forearm on the window and closed his eyes briefly. The good doc was right of course, but something told Alex the stamina would take care of itself with proper training. Speed coupled with speed would only equal the same or greater speed. So long as the foal was born healthy and with solid conformation. Then again, there were plenty of champions with bad legs. It happened. But this all brought him back to the same wall he'd faced for nearly two weeks, and time was up.

"Trip agrees with you. He thinks Beastley for Lockley."

"So does your father."

Alex nodded. Why couldn't he go with the easy answer? Maybe because easy and safe were never going to launch their breeding division the way he needed it to launch. In racing or with his family.

"When do you need to decide?"

Alex walked back to his notebook and flipped to the seventh tab, titled SCHEDULES. His eyes lifted to Dr. Vickers. "I have a call with them tomorrow morning at nine."

"So then, today."

Nodding, he shut the notebook and tucked it under his arm. "Today." Then he started for the door, as Vickers called, asking where he was going.

"I need a little liquid courage."

He smiled. "Don't we all? Give me a yell if you need anything."

Alex smiled back. "You can count on it."

Alex pushed through the door of Rudy's, the bell jingling as he entered, and went to the bar, nodding a hello to the bartender and owner, who as far as Alex knew, arrived at three when the bar opened and didn't return back home until after it closed at two A.M. He wondered how a man of his age could maintain such a schedule, but then he'd never actually seen Rudy take a drink, so maybe it was easier to work late into the evening if you remained sober the whole time.

The bar was empty except for a few regulars, and Rudy was bound to cut them off long before the evening crowd arrived.

"Beer?" Rudy asked.

"Yeah, thanks." Alex laid out his notebook and began poring over every detail of the two horses, desperate to find a piece of information that would make it simple. But there wasn't anything. Both Beastley and Pirate Pete were solid stallions with fantastic pedigrees. Either would make sense, but which made *more* sense? That was the question, the one that had kept Alex up more nights than he could count trying to figure out the puzzle. He thought of his talk with Beckett Carlisle, Emery's father, who went from training to breeding, and how after he'd told Alex everything he thought of it, had sighed heavily and said, "It's a gamble like everything else, son. Sometimes you win, sometimes you lose. All you can do is take the information you've got and make the best decision you can."

Rudy set Alex's beer in front of him, and he took a long pull, then two, before setting it down and diving back into his notes. At this point, his lack of decision was becoming an embarrassment and he knew it. Trip wouldn't say that at the cages, but the truth was, Trip would have made the decision immediately. He was always an act-now, figure-it-out-later kind of person. Which was how he'd agreed to hire Emery, and she'd won the Derby and the Preakness last year, narrowly missing out the Belmont, placing instead of winning. Trip's decisions always went that way, though. He made them so quickly, one would question whether he could possibly be right, but then the outcome was gold. So why couldn't Alex follow his advice now?

"Hey there, handsome. Didn't know you hung around here during daylight hours."

Alex peeked up to find a bright smile and a headful of long curly red hair taking the seat beside him. He peered around, looking for Emery but coming up empty, and flashed her a grin because he couldn't seem to be around her without grinning.

"I think I need a restraining order or something," Kate joked. "Keep seeing you everywhere I go."

"Me? You're in my town." He smiled at her again, enjoying how easily they fell into this carefree banter.

"Ah, I guess you've got me there."

"What are you doing here anyway?" he asked.

"Your soon-to-be sister-in-law. Driving me crazy. She asked me to come in to taste cake samples over at Patty's."

Alex's eyebrows shot up. "She's not having Annie-Jean make her cake?"

"Now you know better than that. Patty and Annie-Jean might have made up after that twenty-year-long fight or whatever, but Annie-Jean's still far too sensitive about it to let Patty get chosen over her. They're doing it together, but Patty had more space or something, now that AJ&P started offering lunch. I don't know."

"So you just ate your weight in sugar. Is that what you're tell-ing me?"

"God," Kate said, rubbing her stomach and causing her shirt to lift a bit, exposing a sliver of skin. Alex swallowed hard. "I might not eat another thing for a week. But I figured I'm already high on one drug, might as well add a second."

At that Alex turned toward her, unable to keep from edging just a little bit closer. "So let me get this straight—your fix to sin is to add more sin? Damn, woman, you're going to be the death of me."

"Hey, now. I can't help my logic. Anyway, what's this?" She reached over for Alex's notebook and slid it in front of her, resting both her elbows on the bar and leaning in close to read.

"You are such a teacher."

"Shh," she said, waving him off.

Alex contemplated telling her none of it would make sense to her, but maybe it would. Hell, maybe she would see it all clearly and know just what he should do.

Finally, after several minutes of him watching her and her *hmm*-ing and *oh*-ing and *I can see that*-ing, she closed the notebook and glanced up at him.

"You can't decide, can you?"

"How did you get that out of my notes?"

Kate tapped her chest. "Teacher here. I know doubt when I see it. But maybe I can help you. Can I meet them?"

Alex peered around the empty bar, then back at her. "Who?"

"Beastley—God, what an awful name—and Pirate Pete. You said I could take a tour anyway." She dropped her gaze and peered up below her eyelashes, batting them for effect. "Show me your stallion, Alex."

He swallowed hard, his stallion definitely hinting that it wanted to come out and play, before she burst out laughing. "Sorry, bad humor."

Swallowing again, Alex reached for his beer and downed the whole thing before turning back to find her watching him. "All right. Let's go."

Chapter Nine

K ate walked out of Rudy's to go to her car, but Alex caught her arm and steered her the other way.

"We'll just take mine. I've gotta pick up something from Mayor Phillips later anyway, so I can bring you back by."

Kate's gaze went to Alex's hand, still on her forearm, and she swallowed hard, unable to look at him for fear she would reveal exactly how much that simple touch affected her. "Okay, what are you in today?"

He nodded to the cherry red Corvette parked a few spots away from them. "That's me."

A smile spread across Kate's face as she walked up to the car and ran her hand gently over the shiny, ultrawaxed exterior. "You fixed her." She remembered seeing the car in his garage all those months ago, parts strewn out all around it.

Alex popped on his shades and stared at the car, but even though his eyes were shaded, she could sense the pride rolling off him.

"Last summer."

He walked over and unlocked the door with his key, then opened it for her. "No auto locks," he said in answer to her raised eyebrows.

"Not that. I just can't believe you're opening a car door."

He grinned. "I think I'd surprise you in a lot of ways if you got to know the real me."

"I think you're right." Their gazes held for a second before Kate forced her mind to work again and slipped into the car. The interior was as red as the exterior, the leather seats shining equally as bright, and Kate found herself comparing it with the gray Jetta with gray interior she'd gotten into the weekend before, and how different it felt for her to sit in this car, how different it felt to sit beside this driver.

Alex stopped to peer around before reversing out of the space and heading out to the main road. The day was warm but not hot, a hint of wind swirling all around them, keeping everything comfortable. Kate expected him to turn left, toward Hamilton Stables, but instead he turned right. "Are you kidnapping me or something?"

He winked. "Don't tempt me."

And Kate thought she wouldn't mind being kidnapped by Alex for a day or two. Or longer, but then she remembered this was Alex— no extended kidnappings to be had.

"Where are we going?"

And then, in answer, he took the next left, and just as she opened her mouth to ask again, he floored it, throwing her back against her seat as a giggle burst from her lips.

Gripping the armrest and her seat, she held on for the ride as Alex raced down the long stretch of back road, cradled by pastures, no one to mind them except the occasional cow.

Adrenaline soared through Kate as her eyes pulled away from the road and over to Alex, a determined expression on his face. Then he peered back at her, and the wild look on his face, free and alive, made her want to tell him to pull over. To take her in his arms and never let go. Risk and future be damned. This man lit her on fire.

A tingly feeling worked through her, and she ached to reach out to take his hand, to feel a bit of the adrenaline rushing through him. But too quickly, he slowed the car and pulled into a dirt road at the end of the road they were on and glanced back at her.

"What did you think? Fast as sin right?"

She grinned. "It's . . ." She shook her head, again afraid her heart would speak for her, especially now when there was no one around, only the trees and the wind and field after field to witness their exchange. To hear her confession. She'd never wanted anything as badly as she wanted Alex, and knowing she couldn't have him made it all that much harder to stay away. Yet she couldn't seem to turn him loose.

Finally, she tilted her head up to peer at the clouds above, her heart still racing in her chest despite the car long since stopping. She didn't want her heart to slow down, didn't want this thrill to end. So she smiled over at Alex and said, "Again. Go again."

As though the words were the exact thing he'd hoped she would say, he leaned over and kissed her on the forehead, then put the car in reverse, and within seconds, they were roaring down the road again, Kate's hair everywhere, her own laughter the only sound she could hear.

"Had enough?" Alex asked as they stopped at the end of the road.

"Never. But you've got a decision to make and I don't want to keep you from that. Let's go meet Beastley and Pete."

Alex's back tensed, and Kate wished she hadn't mentioned anything at all. But she'd always known that decisions were the hardest leading up to the moment you had to make them; then the relief after was some of the best and freest moments of your life. She wanted him to have that moment, wanted to see the carefree Alex before her again, but that wouldn't happen until he worked through this decision, and if she could help him get there, she wanted to try.

"How about we celebrate you making the decision tomorrow night? Braves are playing the Mets. Eight o'clock game. We can get pizza."

Alex's mouth twitched up on one side. "That sounds an awful lot like a date, Ms. Littleton. And shouldn't teachers date nice guys?"

"First, not a date. A celebration between friends. And second . . ." She paused until he glanced over at her. "You are a nice guy."

His mouth set into an even line as he stared at her, his hands still wrapped around the steering wheel, shades over his eyes, and for once she wished she could see his eyes so she would know what he was thinking. Just as she began to ask, he said, "No one has ever seen me the way you see me."

Kate drew a slow breath, once again pushing away those thoughts and feelings she shouldn't have. "Maybe they weren't looking. People see what they want to see. To truly see a person's core takes more effort, but I've never felt it was right to do anything less with the people you care about. You shouldn't just see them. You should look, pay attention. Else you might miss something. Something special."

Biting his lip in that way Kate loved, Alex flexed his hands around the steering wheel, his head fixing straight on the road, then back at her, like he didn't know which way to go—to the farm or directly to her lips. "Damn Trip."

Craning around, Kate searched for her best friend's fiancé, but the only set of eyes she met were of a dark brown cow in a pasture beside her, his expression filled with boredom. "What?"

"Nothing. Just I agreed to something with Trip that I'm now wishing I could get out of."

He turned right onto a main street, his back tighter than it had been before.

"What sort of something?"

Kate noticed him working his bottom lip between his teeth the way he did when he was overthinking something, and she reached over to tug his jaw down, gently releasing the lip. His breath rushed through his teeth in a quick hiss, then he peered over. "You can't do that. I'll never be able to keep this up if you touch me."

"What?" Kate repeated, sure she'd stepped into the middle of a conversation instead of the beginning.

"I'll try the friend thing. Hell, obviously I can't stay away from you, so might as well try something. But you can't touch me. Especially not like that. Damn." He shook his head once, then peered over at her. "And no looking at me like that."

Kate raised her hands in a you-lost-me-again gesture. "Like what?"

"Like you want to take my clothes off. Cows around be damned."

"I do not."

"You do. And I can't have it. Not right now. So I'll be your friend. Hell, I'll be your best friend, and you can call me about work problems and sad commercials you watch and dates and—scratch that. No date talk. But everything else is game. No touching and no looks, though, Red, got that? Please, for my sanity."

Kate's brows lifted. "No. Sorry. I'm not even sure we're having the same conversation. Or any conversation for that matter. What are you talking about?"

"I made a vow of celibacy," Alex half-yelled at the next stoplight, receiving a sharp look from the convertible beside them. He waved a hello like it wasn't anything, then eyed Kate. "I can't go there, Red. I vowed to be a good boy until I have everything in order, and God knows how long that will take. And every time you touch me or look at me in that way you like to do—"

"The I-want-to-take-your-clothes-off look?" Kate offered.

"Exactly. Every time you do that, I want to say to shit with the job and my brother and whoever the hell else and take you in this car. Here and now, consequences be damned. But I can't do that. I've worked for eighteen months to get this all in order and I'm this close." He pinched his forefinger and thumb together. He drew a quick breath, clearly getting more and more revved up, so Kate reached over and pressed her hand to his thigh, hoping to calm him, but instead he jumped back, his eyes smoldering as they hit hers.

"Woman, did you hear what I said? No looks. No touching." His gaze dropped and he groaned loudly. "I must be a freaking saint."

A smile played at Kate's lips, but she pushed it away, not wanting him to think she was laughing at him. "Okay."

"Okay what?"

"Okay, we can be friends. I want to be your friend. I like being around you. You make me laugh and you're fun. I promise no looks and no touching." She slowly lifted her hand and held it out as if in evidence, then dramatically placed it in her own lap. "Better?"

He released a breath, then two, and Kate had to fight from smiling again. It was nice to see that she got him that keyed up. "Much."

"Good. Now, friend, take me to meet these horses. It's nearing the end of the day and you have a decision to make."

Alex turned into Hamilton Stables, his jaw set. "That I do."

Alex parked the Corvette in his garage and walked around to open the door for Kate, but she was already stepping out.

"Golf cart?"

"A step down, I know, but it's the easiest way to get around the farm."

"You don't have to explain everything to me all the time. I'm not one of those people."

Alex sat down in the driver's seat and nodded for her to climb in. "I know you're not."

They drove down Alex's drive and out to the main road that connected each of the divisions of Hamilton Stables. Though Alex knew Kate had been there before, he didn't think she'd been around the farm, so he took his time, pointing out the foaling barn, the stallion barn, the training section of the farm, where horses Trip was actively working were stabled, and then the track, which always impressed tourists who visited the farm. But Kate wasn't staring at the track; she was staring at him with that damn look of hers that always showed exactly what she was thinking.

"We've talked about this," he said.

"What?"

"You're giving me that look again."

"I am not."

"You are. Those eyes that take in every one of my features. Drives me insane."

"I'm not thinking about undressing you. Right now, at least." She winked, and Alex groaned, causing the smile to slip away from her. "That was just a joke. Innocent flirting."

"No such thing."

"Fine. No flirting, but I wasn't thinking about that. I was thinking that you seem really proud. Of the farm. Of your family and what they've accomplished here. Even when you spoke about the track, I could tell you were really proud of Trip for building it all from the ground up."

Alex shrugged. "They're my family."

Kate nodded slowly. "They are. So maybe you should trust that they see you more clearly than you think they do. Then trust yourself enough to make this decision and stand by it. Be firm and hold true to yourself and you can't go wrong."

"It isn't that easy."

"It is. Has every horse Trip has ever trained become a champion?"

Alex stilled, his mind going to the horses that had been champions, but there were far more that weren't. Trip had had as many as four horses in any given Derby. Only one could win. "No."

"But people keep coming back to him, right? That's because he oozes confidence. They trust him because he's sure of what he does and follows through as best he can. But he'll never reach one hundred percent. No one can."

A smile tugged at Alex's lips as he leaned over the steering wheel and peered over at Kate. "You're pretty smart, you know that? You should become a teacher when you grow up."

Kate rolled her eyes. "Ha ha. Now stop delaying. It's almost four. Broodmares, then stallions."

"Why the mares first?"

"I have to see the ladies first. How else am I supposed to figure out their matches?"

Alex spun the golf cart around and headed in the opposite direction. "Here I was thinking I needed to look at the stud books, when really all I needed was to call in a matchmaker." He slapped the steering wheel dramatically. "Why didn't I think of that before?" he joked.

But as they parked outside the boarding barn and Kate started down the center, stopping at each of the ten stalls and greeting the mares like they were old friends, he began to wonder if maybe he should have sought her out weeks ago. She spoke in hushed whispers to the horses, each of them coming over at her words, as though she had hold of their reins and drew them to her instead of the words alone provoking their movement.

"You didn't tell me you grew up on a farm."

Kate lifted her gaze to meet Alex's before returning to the mare before her. "I'm from Crestler's Key. Everyone either owns a farm or works on one."

"You didn't want to work on your family's farm after you graduated?"

She shrugged. "My brothers do, but I always wanted to teach. I used to pretend to teach my dolls when I was little. I guess it stuck."

Alex leaned in behind her, tapping on the stall, causing her to suck in her breath either from the sudden closeness or the sound, he wasn't sure. "This is one of the McKendricks' mares. Lockley. The other is Tyrant Queen, there." He pointed to the middle stall across from them. "If this goes well, the McKendricks will board all their mares here, and train the weanlings here, too."

"They don't want to sell them?"

Alex nodded. "Some. But the McKendricks like trophies. They'll sell half, keep half."

"How do they decide which to keep and which to sell?"

Alex's chin lifted a fraction of an inch, but he needed it before he said his next words. "Me."

"You decide which they keep and sell? What if you sell one that becomes a champion and keep one that doesn't?"

Walking over to a stable boy who was coming into the barn, Alex shook his hand and motioned around the stalls, asking the young man to change out the soiled hay. "They're my clients. I can't control who goes across the finish line first—that's on Trip—but if I do my job right, they'll keep champions and sell champions."

"Seems like a lot of pressure. No wonder you gave up sex."

At that, the stable boy released a hiccupped laugh and Alex glared at Kate. "Thank you," he whispered.

She grinned back. "Hey, I didn't force you into celibacy. Blame your brother."

Now the boy was outright boiled over laughing, unable to stop.

"All right. We're done here." He motioned for Kate to get back into the golf cart. "Thank you. Now all of the farm will think the Hamilton brothers are into some freaky shit."

Kate beamed back at him. "You're not? Then maybe I could help you with that. Show you a few things. I *am* a teacher after all."

"Like I said: You're going to be the death of me, woman."

They reached the stallion barn, all white with black trim, only five stalls inside, four of them filled. The stalls themselves were gated with black swirling iron, beautiful and strong. Alex had supervised its construction himself and was tremendously proud of it.

Kate walked in and without a word started for the last stall on the right. Her head dropped down and she reached a hand out to stroke the name engraved into the plate in the center of the stall's door. "Pirate Pete." The words were spoken in a whisper, and as she lifted her gaze to take in the bay horse before her, Alex found himself holding back, stopping several feet away, watching as Kate stared at the horse. He expected her to begin speaking to the stallion as she had the mares, but instead she just continued to stare, each second drawing long, and suddenly, instead of wondering what she was thinking or what she would say, he found himself staring at her, tracing the lines of her face. The swirl and spin of her curly hair. The straight line of her back, forever in perfect posture, the swell of her breasts and hips. His mind drifted back to their night together, how sure she'd been of herself, and how the night had gone on and on, Alex unable to get enough of her.

He leaned against the stable door and continued to watch her, his heart picking up speed for reasons that had nothing to do with his decision and everything to do with the fiery woman before him and how easily she fit in his world. As acquaintance. As lover. As friend. It made him wonder if in time she could be more.

Finally, Kate ran her fingers over Pirate Pete's nameplate again and stepped away, her face unreadable. The stallion reacted as strangely, whinnying as she left his stall, and Alex thought he saw a bit of hurt cross her face before she went to the next horse, then the next, finally landing in front of Beastley. Immediately, Alex could tell she didn't share the connection with the prize stallion that she did with Pete, and once again, Alex wanted to question her on it, but he kept back, letting her do her thing. Letting her get to know the horses in her own way.

After several minutes of staring at Beastley as she had Pete, she stepped away, but not toward Alex; she went to each of the other stallions.

"The last stall is open."

Alex took a step toward her, but immediately he felt as though he'd invaded a private conversation not meant for his ears. "It's for Craving Wind."

She peered over. "Emery's horse?"

"Yes. He'll retire in another six months to become a stud. With him winning the Derby and Preakness, his fee will be large and his offspring will bring a lot of money to the farm."

"Seems sad."

"What?"

"That it's all about money."

At that, Alex stepped up beside her, sure now what had caused her reaction. How hadn't he seen it before? She didn't agree with the treatment of the horses, and Alex would bet the jockeys didn't either. Racing was a grueling sport, not for the faint of heart, and an animal lover could easily find fault in their practices. Hamilton Stables pushed for moral and sound treatment of all their staff and animals, but certain sides of racing were unavoidable.

Like breeding.

A stallion might have fifty or a hundred coverings in so many months, every year, until he was too old to continue. It was a business, a much more profitable business than racing. But knowing that and explaining it were two entirely different things.

Instead, he said, "It is." Because it was true.

"Why do you do it?"

"Why do you teach? It's who I am, what I was raised to be. And while I won't say it's perfect, these animals were born to race, Kate. Watch a mare foal and the colt stumble up immediately, ready to run even before he knows how to walk, and you'll know what I mean."

Kate drew a long breath and focused back on the horse before her—Gaelic Thunder—and she nodded once. "This is your match for Lockley. Pete gets Tyrant Queen."

Alex scratched his head and peered around, eyeing each of the nameplates and horses before his gaze landed on the word *Beastley*. He couldn't imagine telling Trip and the McKendricks that he was excluding the farm's best stallion.

"I can't throw Gaelic into the mix. Beastley has sired more champions than any other stallion in this stable. Three times more."

Kate shrugged. "Do you have three mares boarded for the McKendricks or just two?"

"Two."

She shrugged again. "Then you'll just have to leave him out."

Alex laughed. "You're crazy, you know that?"

"I'm right," she said without a hint of humor. "Trust me or don't, but I'm right. I know how people and animals work. It's one of the reasons I became a teacher. I like to meet a student and work out what it takes to help him or her learn. This isn't really very different. I've met your mares and your stallions and I'm telling you what I think."

"You barely looked at their pedigrees."

"You're the one who said it's a mistake to trust paper alone."

Alex walked around the stable, allowing his focus to move from Kate to outside. He couldn't think when she was in his line of sight. "Yeah, but you can't just say hello to a horse and think you know which mare to cross with which stallion."

"I didn't just say hello. I also looked over their conformation. Pedigree is one thing, but Beastley has calf knees. You're lucky it hasn't shown in any of his offspring, but it will eventually, and then you've just knowingly bred a horse that will in all likelihood get injured during a race and retire before he's even fully begun his career."

Turning to look at her, his mouth falling slack, Alex asked, "You didn't tell me you knew so much about Thoroughbreds."

"Emery's been my best friend for a long time, which meant I spent a lot of time around Carlisle Farms. I paid attention."

Alex walked over to Beastley's stall and eyed his legs. She was right. He'd never considered Beastley's less than perfect conformation because it had never been a problem for the stallion when he was actively racing, and so far none of his offspring had inherited it. So far.

He spun around to face her. "How do you exist?" he breathed.

"Well, see, when my mother married my father, they chose to consummate, which can sometimes produce offspring." She pointed at herself. "Evidence of said process working."

Alex smiled as he started for her, unable to stay away, unable to keep up this pretense that he didn't want this woman in his arms. He told himself he was strong enough to be friends with her, to touch her and flirt without fear of losing his focus, and he saw no reason not to test his resolve. Reaching for her hands, he glided his fingers through hers and tugged her close, her head resting on his chest as he wrapped his arms around her, hugging her to him. Taking a slow breath and relishing the mixture of flowers and soap and something else he couldn't quite make out, he allowed his eyes to close and rested his chin on her head Then, with an impressive amount of strength, he took a step back, unwilling to look at her, for if he did and he saw in her eyes the same surge of passion he felt in his chest, he'd have no choice but to cover her mouth with his and forget the rest.

"Thank you," he said simply. "I'll take you back to your car now."

Kate stood in place, still not moving, even as Alex stepped outside. Drawing one long breath, he peeked up at her, his hair in his eyes, hoping to hide the sheer desire he felt. And then his gaze met hers and he knew she was facing the same struggle as he.

"Kate?"

She shook her head, breaking the spell, and dropped her chin, before following after him. "Coming."

Six months, Alex told himself. *Be good for six months and then you can have her*. But what if six months was too long? What if she found someone else?

His phone buzzed just as he started the golf cart, and he glanced down to see Trip's name flashing back at him. "Give me a second?" he asked Kate.

"Sure."

The sun hung low in the sky, and though Alex never wore a watch, he knew the time was approaching five fast. Trip wanted a decision. Walking over to a nearby tree, Alex leaned against it and stared out over the farm, the expanse of fields, the staff working away in every barn. This decision was greater than him and his pride. The continued success of the farm rested on his shoulders.

"Hey," Alex said, taking the call.

"Well?"

Alex scrubbed his jaw with his hand, then shoved that hand in his pocket. "I've decided."

Trip released a breath, which grated on Alex's nerves. Did he really think Alex wouldn't decide? That he'd let this go on forever?

"Are you going to share this decision, or do I need to try to decode it from your shallow breathing? Where are you anyway?"

"At the stallion barn."

"So you have decided."

"That's what I said, isn't it?"

"And?"

"Before I tell you, how would you cross them?"

Trip hesitated on the other end, maybe wondering if Alex was still unsure, but it wasn't that at all. He wanted his brother to say out loud how he would do it, so when Alex did the opposite, Trip would have no choice but to admit that Alex had been right.

"What did Vickers say?" Trip asked.

"Queen with Beastley. Lockley with Pete."

"I agree."

Alex nodded to himself. Of course he did.

"But it doesn't matter what I think," Trip continued. "It matters what you think. It's your call."

A surge of pride rocketed through him. It was the first time Trip had ever put his full faith in Alex and he didn't want to let him down. Alex told himself to go with their choices, but they had never felt right to him. He'd known all along that he wanted Queen crossed with Pete. To hear Kate agree had brought on more relief than he would ever admit. Lockley would then be expected to cross with Beastley, and that was where Alex had planned to put her before Kate's mention of his calf knees.

"I'll call you back," Alex said.

"What? Tell me your choice."

"I'll tell you after I call the McKendricks."

He hung up before his brother could argue and called Tom Mc-Kendrick, who answered on the first ring. "Tom, it's Alex Hamilton. I wanted to discuss your broodmares and the studs I've chosen for them."

"Go ahead."

Alex inhaled once; then, trusting himself, he said, "Tyrant Queen will couple with Pirate Pete."

"And Lockley?"

Alex turned around to face the golf cart, to face Kate. "Gaelic Thunder."

Chapter Ten

"Miss Littleton. I had an accident."

Kate peered down at the little girl before her, Suzy, her favorite student, though she would never admit to having a favorite. All day her thoughts had been on Alex and their pizza date that night, or pizza hangout, or whatever it was. There would be pizza and baseball and Alex, and despite telling herself to keep it casual, she was excited.

Suzy's dark hair was pulled back into two split braids, and across her dark cheeks were splotches of white paint. "Uh-oh. What happened?" Kate asked, wiping one of the splotches with her fingertips, which did little more than spread it more.

Suzy pointed to the left, and Kate's gaze followed the little girl's outstretched hand to a paint can, turned over, white paint spilling out everywhere onto the asphalt.

"Eek!" Kate screamed, which made the little girl's bottom lip tremble.

"I'm so sorry. It just turned over, and I tried to sit it back up, but it fell over again and I couldn't get it to stop, and my clothes and—"

"Shh, calm down, honey." Kate hugged the girl, resulting in two little white handprints on Kate's red T-shirt. Suzy's gaze dropped and her eyes teared up again. "It's fine. Really."

She draped an arm around the little girl and directed her toward the paint. Bending down, she tried to set the can up, and sure enough it fell right back over. "Hmm."

"See. I wasn't lying. It won't stay."

Kate patted the girl's head, which then placed a Kate-sized white handprint on her head. Cringing, Kate pulled away, but the damage was done. To tell her and risk full-out tears or let it go?

"Oh! Maggie's here." Suzy ran off to join her friend, and Kate released a slow breath. What was she thinking, allowing a bunch of third graders to paint something this big? But then she turned around to see them all working together on the set, laughing and acting out various scenes from the play, and she smiled. She might get fired for this, but at least these kids would always remember the fun they had.

"Who earned that smile? I'd like to go get a few pointers."

Kate's grin widened as she peered over her shoulder at Alex. Today he wore a Braves cap and shades, a fitted black T-shirt, and loose gym shorts. She wondered if he ever looked rough. Didn't he have off days, when his hair didn't work right or he had breakouts or something?

"And now you glare at me? I'm here to help you."

"Sorry, I'm just jealous of your face."

Alex leaned in and pressed his cheek to hers. "Well, here, take some. I'll share." Kate laughed and pushed his face away. "God, you're ridiculous."

He winked. "Only around you, Red. Now, where do you want me?" He flexed his arms. "These muscles are ready to work."

"I'm pretty sure there's a joke in there somewhere, but I'm going to let it go in the name of innocent ears." Kate motioned to the kids.

"Admit it: You like having me around."

Suddenly, Kate's heartbeat became very noticeable, her skin humming under his stare. "Too much."

Alex nodded slowly, as though he, too, enjoyed her company a little too much. "Are we still on for tonight?"

"Pizza and baseball? You couldn't ditch me if you tried."

"Ditch you from what?" a quieter and decidedly female voice called from behind Kate.

She turned to find Emery standing a few feet away, and immediately Kate blushed. Had Emery heard their flirting? Would she tell Trip? And then it occurred to her that for the first time in her life she was hiding something from her best friend. It had less to do with Emery and more to do with Emery's fiancé, but still . . . The realization made her chest ache, and now she wondered how much of a lie she would have to tell to protect Alex from Trip's wrath. But then, before she had to say anything, Alex said, "We're painting another section of the set. It's Kate's favorite part." Then he nodded toward the two parents working to nail up the tower and failing miserably. "I'd better go rescue them from themselves."

"Thanks," Kate said, hoping he knew it was for more than just the parents or Emery. It was for everything. He'd helped tremendously with the set, suffering through all the chaos that often came with managing twenty-two eight-year-olds and always having a smile on his face. She loved working with her students, but knowing Alex would be there, too, made her heart race every time she arrived at the school to work.

Once he was out of earshot, Emery leaned in close. "What was that about?"

And here was the problem with hiding something from someone who'd known you most of your life. They sensed all the things you refused to say.

"What?"

"Alex. He's helping here. Enjoying it even," she said, tossing a hand in his direction. "He's changed, I think. The Alex I met eighteen months ago only thought of himself."

"Or maybe you didn't know him very well."

Emery's eyebrows threaded together. "Kate, you just defended a boy."

"A man."

"Fine, a man. You just defended a man."

Kate turned away from her friend, sure she knew exactly where this was going and wanting no part of it. "So?"

"So, you are the eternal feminist. Girl can do all, does not need a man. I've never heard you defend a man in your life that wasn't your father or your brother, and they're blood. And you appeared to be in pain both times you defended them. Both as in two times. In your whole life. What's going on?"

"Nothing."

"Nothing my ass. You're my best friend. You're really not going to tell me?"

Kate dropped the paint can she was holding back into the box full of a dozen more paint cans, half of them empty now because Tommy Jeffers thought it would be funny to paint one of the buses. God, she was so getting fired.

"Kate?"

Turning, she tossed up her hands. "I like him, okay? And I know I shouldn't, and I know it's stupid, and I know he'll probably break my heart. But I do. I like him. And we're kind of friends. And I like it. He's funny and nice and he makes me smile and laugh and I don't want to give it up, okay?"

Emery's eyes were wide, but she said nothing.

"Okay?"

"Okay."

Kate crossed her arms and shot her friend the scrutinizing stare she'd mastered in the classroom. "You want to say something."

Emery sealed her lips and shook her head, which did little more than cause Kate to roll her eyes. "Spill it already or I'll worry all night over what you refused to say."

"Fine, but you asked me to." Then she peered around to make sure no one was close by. "This is Alex we're talking about. He doesn't exactly ooze commitment. Are you sure you want to go there?"

"Yes."

"You didn't even think about it."

At that, Kate laughed. "Are you joking? I've done nothing *but* think about it. Eighteen months of thinking and trying out different guys. Trying to find someone who would make me feel half as alive as he does. And you know what? It hasn't worked. So I'm trying something else now."

"Friendship."

"Yes; why's that so hard to believe?" Kate considered yelling at her friend, but Emery would just yell back, and there were the kids to consider. That was the thing about their relationship—Emery had no problem throwing it right back at Kate. She refused to allow her to get away with anything. Which was one of a thousand reasons why she loved her best friend. And normally, she would listen to her, or at least pretend to. But Emery was getting married now, tilting the scale and leaving Kate behind. Eventually they would no longer talk on the phone for an hour and go shopping for half a day and return with nothing. She'd be busy doing married things, like hosting cocktail parties and entertaining. Plus—and it hurt a little to admit this—Emery didn't understand Alex. She didn't see him the way Kate saw him, so it was useless to try to convince her of anything. Still, she had to at least show her point.

"It's like that dress thing that popped up on Facebook. Some swore it was black and others swore it was blue, and you couldn't convince either side of anything, when in reality the dress was probably yellow and both sides were wrong."

Emery's expression creased in confusion. "What? Are you comparing Alex to a dress?"

Sighing, Kate glanced over to where Alex was showing two boys how to hammer a nail. The tender way he walked them through it but still stepped back a bit to let them pretend to be men. He was good to the core. Why couldn't others see that?

"I like him. I'm just asking you not to make it a thing. I'll worry about my heart. You worry about your wedding."

Emery cocked her head and watched her friend for another minute before sighing heavily. "Fine, but if he breaks your heart, I'm going to skin him alive."

Kate smiled. "Noted. Now why are you here? Something tells me it has nothing to do with Alex."

"Oh, right. I wanted your opinion on invitations. We have to make the decision this week. Which do you like better?" Emery pulled out two ivory vintage-looking invitations, which as best Kate could tell were exactly the same.

She studied the paper, the font, the gold raised lettering, then lifted her gaze to her friend. "Am I missing something here?"

"You're joking right? They're completely different."

Kate raised one closer to her face, then the other, curious if maybe there was some small detail you could only see up close, but again, she saw no difference at all. She handed them back to her friend. "I choose that one." She tapped the one on top. "It's more you."

Emery cocked an eyebrow at her. "You still don't see the difference, do you?"

"No clue."

"Kate!"

"They're both fine, Em. You can't go wrong here. Plus, if I don't see the difference, maybe I'm not the best person to ask."

"You're the maid of honor."

Kate laughed. "Yes, well, that *honor* title can be a little deceiving."

Just then, Kate noticed a Mercedes pulling up and Nick stepping out and starting over toward Alex. She thought he might ask Alex to go with him somewhere, which made Kate sadder than it should, but instead he went to work beside him.

"He called Nick to help."

"What? Who—oh." Emery followed her gaze. "Yeah, he probably would've called Trip, too, if they weren't arguing right now."

"They're arguing?"

Emery nodded. "Something about the McKendricks' mares. Alex went a different way from what Trip felt he should have done."

Kate watched Alex work, watched him laughing with Nick. "Do you know what his decision was?" Could it be that he went with her advice over his brother's?

"No idea, but Trip was livid. I'm sure they'll get over it soon, though. Trip needs to trust Alex more. Maybe he'll fail. But maybe he'll really, really succeed, too, you know?"

Kate looked at her friend. "I didn't think you liked Alex."

"I like him. He's going to be my brother-in-law. I just don't think he's good enough for you."

"I love you," Kate said, reaching to hug Emery. "I'm glad you're my best friend, and I'm sorry I didn't tell you about my feelings sooner. I just don't want it to get awkward. Plus, nothing's going to come of it. We're just friends."

"Pretty sure we passed awkward a long time ago. And don't look now, but Mr. I Like Him But He's Just My Friend is staring at you."

Unable to keep from checking, she glanced up and locked eyes with Alex. A small smile played at his lips, but as their gazes held, the smile spread to take over his face. And though Kate knew her feelings were spiraling out of her control, she didn't care. For once, she didn't care.

"I'm off. See you tomorrow?" Emery asked.

Kate broke her stare down with Alex to look at her. "What's tomorrow?"

"Bridesmaids' dresses. Did you forget?"

"No, of course not." Yes, totally. Somehow Kate's brain wasn't working like it should, and throw in how often her mind drifted to Alex and all the possibilities there, and suddenly other parts of her were doing the thinking—or lack of thinking.

"You'll be there, right? We're just going to that shop in Triple Run. Please tell me you're coming. Mama's insisting on being there after

missing the first wedding dress thing. She'll have a thousand opinions, all of them horrible. If you're not there, you'll end up wearing
canary yellow with matching hats or something."

Kate blanched.

"I know. You have to be there."

"Don't worry, I'm there. No canary yellow in your wedding, I
promise."

Emery beamed at her and kissed her cheek. "I'm so lucky to
have you."

"Yes, you are. Now, either get to work or head on. I have a mess of
kids to keep busy." She winked at Emery, who waved goodbye. Then,
once she was out of view, Kate started toward the man who was still
staring at her, a wicked smile on his face as she approached.

"What are you staring at?"

He swiped away a bead of sweat from his forehead, causing his
shirt to lift, exposing a sliver of skin that looked far too enticing for
such young eyes to be around. "I'm pretty sure everyone here knows
what I'm staring at. The question is, what are you staring at? Are you
going to finally admit to checking me out or are we going to keep up
this dance?"

"I'm not dancing."

"You're dancing. And I like it. But I'm eager to find out what our
next step is." His lips twitched. "So what's our next step, Red?"

"I . . ."

"Hey, do you have any more nails?" Nick asked as he approached,
clamping his brother hard on the shoulder, as if in warning.

Alex cursed under his breath and peered up. "Fantastic timing. As
always."

"I try." Nick flashed Kate a grin. "How are you?"

"Good; you?"

"I'm fantastic."

"Thanks for coming by to help. Not sure where we'd be without
so many coming to help." Her eyes fell on Alex before she could stop
them, and suddenly the warm April heat turned scorching. Tiny beads
of sweat dotted his temples and spots on his T-shirt, and never in her
life had she viewed sweat as so unbelievably sexy.

Nick's gaze followed hers. "Well, it's nice to help once in a while.
As long as we keep it fun; right, brother?"

Alex focused back on the piece of the set he was hammering. "Right, fun."

Nick walked away and Kate watched him go. Why did it seem like he was talking about her and Alex?

"What was that about?"

Alex hammered the nail in place. "Ah, you know, family stuff."

"It kind of seemed like he was talking about us."

"That's because he was."

Kate focused on Alex, sure she'd heard him wrong. "What?"

"Trip isn't the only one against us hanging out."

"So Nick . . . ?"

"Nick thinks you're a good girl."

"What exactly does he think you are?"

"Well, not a good girl, that's for sure." Alex laughed.

"You know what I mean."

He stared back at her. "I do."

"Then tell me what this is about. First Trip, then Emery, and now Nick?"

"They're just trying to protect you."

Kate placed her hands on her hips. "Yeah, well, I'm a big girl. I can look out for myself. I can do anything I like, whenever the freaking hell I like."

Just then, Kate heard a series of gasps from behind her, and she turned slowly to see Suzy and Maggie behind her, their hands over their mouths, their eyes wide.

"Ms. Littleton!"

"Oh—no, I wasn't—I didn't mean to . . ." Oh my God.

And just when she'd prepared to apologize to her students for cussing in front of them, Alex reached into the pail of soapy water and sponges they kept there for cleanup and then, before Kate could run, he grabbed her and squeezed one of the sponges over her head. "Water fight!" he called. And suddenly, all the students took off for one of the five buckets positioned around the field where they were working, and sponges were being squeezed over heads, water was being thrown, and laughter filled the air. Suzy and Maggie took off running as two boys from Kate's class ran after them with a bucket full of water, her cussing episode long forgotten.

Kate turned where she stood in Alex's arms and pressed a kiss to his cheek. "Thank you. I know the whole no-touching thing, but I couldn't help it."

He smirked back. "I just squeezed soapy water onto your head."

Kate wiped some of the water out of her eyes. "I know what you did. What you continue to do for me. And I just want you to know it doesn't go unnoticed. I see you, Alex Hamilton. Whether you want to be seen or not."

Now if only she could convince her heart to see them as just friends. *Yeah right.*

"Hey there, gorgeous," Alex said as he opened his front door to let Kate in. She was wearing a Braves jersey and short leggings, her hair swept up high on her head. As far as he could tell, her face was baby clean, without a stitch of makeup.

"Hey, now, if I can't touch you, you can't flirt with me," she said, pointing at him. And then walked on in and took a seat in the center of his large leather couch, kicking off her flip-flops and tucking her legs up under her.

"Comfortable?" he asked with a laugh.

She flashed him a smile. "I'll be more comfortable once you get me a beer."

He grinned back, enjoying the easiness between them, and once he was halfway to the kitchen, out of direct view, he allowed himself to stare at her, unable to stop. Plenty of women had walked through his front door. Plenty had seen his bed and plenty had seen him naked. But none of them had ever felt right in his house, in his world. Like he'd flipped through a catalogue and ordered the woman who would be his best match. It was both unsettling and exhilarating. Something he would love to explore, if only he could go there. Again, he wondered if she would wait. Maybe if he asked, if he explained, she would wait. Or maybe—

"And no staring." Kate's gaze cut over to him before returning to the game.

Alex laughed loudly this time and tossed up his hands. "Damn, call a spade a spade why don't you?"

"I did."

"I know. That's what I said."

"Well, why don't you do as I ask and stop staring and fetch me a beer?"

"Testy as all hell."

Kate grinned. "You like it."

He grinned back. "I do."

Still grinning as he slipped into the kitchen, he grabbed a beer and returned, unsure if he should sit in his La-Z-Boy (safe) or beside her (stupid). Never one to play it safe with Kate, he plopped down beside her but pushed the reclining section of the couch out so at least he had a little distance between himself and her. Still, he couldn't help taking in that all-Kate scent he loved and the easy way she watched the game. Like she couldn't care less what he thought of her. Why didn't women realize that was what made a woman appealing? Anyone could slather on makeup, throw on a sexy outfit, and call herself attractive. But it took something more to walk into a man's house with your hair on top of your head, a baggy jersey covering up your goods, not a lick of makeup, and still look beautiful.

"So unbelievably beautiful."

"What?" She turned to look at him and he shook his head. Clearly he needed to slow his alcohol intake or he'd confess every thought he had about her before the end of the night.

"Nothing."

"Did you order pizza?"

"I can now." He reached across her for his cell, lying innocently on the cushion beside her, but as his body made contact with hers, a jolt hit him, spreading out in all the wrong (and right) places, mixing with the alcohol in his veins, short-circuiting his brain.

Kate drew a sharp breath, her mouth falling open, and his gaze dropped down to her full bottom lip, shiny as though she'd just licked it, and he wondered what it would taste like if he were just to . . .

Without thinking, he leaned in, his gaze flicking up to her eyes and then back to that lip, tempting him.

"Alex."

"Hmm?" He couldn't pull his eyes away now that he'd locked in on her lips. Like a junkie and his next fix, he had to kiss her, had to taste and explore her mouth. Another inch and he'd have all he needed. He'd be able to breathe again.

"Alex."

With considerable effort, he lifted his gaze. "*Kate.* See, I can say your name, too."

"You're not only staring but you're leaning. And not just any lean. *The* lean."

He didn't move, still unable to gain control of his body. "I'm not leaning," he said, even as he leaned a bit closer, her breath hitting his face, and damn it all to hell. One more breath and he was going to say *screw it all* and take that mouth of hers. No asking, just taking.

"No, now you're preparing to kiss me. And we can't kiss."

Alex licked his lips and she stilled. "Maybe you can't kiss, but I can kiss, and I'm happy to show you if you'd like. We'll call it a lesson. Nothing serious and no rules broken."

God, why did she have to look so sexy and cute at the same time? It was taking all his effort not to pull her into his lap, loosen her hair so those curls could fall around her face, and have his way with her. A man shouldn't have to sit this close to a beautiful woman who wanted him without being able to have her.

"All right, Mr. Cocky. I don't need a lesson."

Alex shook his head slowly. "No . . . you don't. If I remember correctly, you could be giving lessons yourself. In fact, that works for my logic, too." He edged closer, tempting her. "Give me a lesson. Teach me, teacher. Hell, at this point I'll even pay you for the lesson. Teachers tutor right? Tutor me." He let his lips brush against hers, barely anything, a silent breeze instead of a forceful wind, but the impact was immediate. Kate slid a hand over his forearm, still crossing her body, the move slow and deliberate, but the expression on her face told Alex that she could no more control her hand than he could control his lips.

"You said no touching, and kissing certainly counts as touching. This counts as touching." Her other hand came up to lightly touch his face, and without thinking, he closed his eyes, basking in the contentment that single touch brought him. How long had it been since a woman made him feel better? Not just a release or a thrill but better? Happier?

He couldn't remember another woman ever making him feel that way, and now that he realized that simple fact, he found himself craving it—desperate for another touch.

The announcer called a home run, and Kate pushed Alex's face out of the way so she could see, causing him to burst into laughter. An ordinary woman would kill a man for doing the same thing, but nothing about Kate was ordinary.

"Bryant hit a homer with two on base. Braves up three," she said, her eyes fixed on the screen before darting back to Alex.

"I don't care."

Kate focused on him. "I know, but maybe you should. You know, think about something else. Take a breath. Whatever you have to do to keep from making a mistake."

"Nothing with you could ever be a mistake."

"You made a vow."

Alex tucked a loose curl behind her ear, allowing his fingertips to glide over her earlobe and down the back of her bare neck. A shiver rippled through her.

"Maybe I can keep my agreement and explore this, too."

"I don't want to cause you any problems. You're so close. You just made the call on Pete and Gaelic."

Alex's head jerked. "How did you know my decision?"

"Emery."

"Ah."

Alex could only guess the conversation Trip had had with his fiancée, likely screaming about Alex's horrible decision and how he was going to tank Hamilton Stables. And maybe he was right. Alex might fail. But at least if he failed, he would fail making his own damn decisions.

"I think we should watch the game," Kate said, but she made no effort to move.

Alex stroked the back of her neck gently, sending another shiver rippling through her. "I think you should kiss me. Or I can kiss you. Either way, there should be kissing."

"Alex . . ."

"You said that already. Give me something else. Anything, Red. Honestly, I'll let you talk me out of this if you try. But I'm a competitive man and right now the win is in sight, and damn"—He bit his lip as his gaze dropped back down to her mouth—"I want the win."

"I'm not willing to be one of many."

"No one is asking you to be. I'm just asking you to wait for me. Spend time with me now; we'll keep it easy and casual. Do whatever you like, whenever you like. But save the finale for me."

Kate slipped her fingers into his hair, gently massaging his scalp. "So you're saying you're keeping your vow of celibacy, but you want to hang out with me. And only me?"

"Plus kissing."

A grin played at her lips. "Plus kissing."

He matched her stroke for stroke, her in his hair, him at the base of her neck, gliding up to her crown and back, until her eyes fluttered closed. "And if I say yes, what then?" The words were breathy and full of meaning. She was asking what their next step would be. What happened after he succeeded—or failed?

"I don't know. All I know is that if I don't kiss you now I'm going to go crazy."

Her eyes flicked open, and in them he saw a new determination. "So kiss me."

"Yeah?"

"Kiss me."

All the permission he needed. Alex gripped her neck and pulled her to him, his mouth covering hers, the connection so intense and so immediate a groan escaped his mouth at the same moment that she moaned against his lips. Needing her closer, he pulled her onto his lap and forced himself to slow down. If this was all they could do, he wanted to take his time and do it right. He wanted this kiss to be etched into her memory, forever a part of her, able to be conjured at will. To take her right back to this moment.

Her lips parted, inviting him in, and he took advantage, slipping his tongue into her mouth and slowly intertwining it with hers, then showing attention to the rest of her mouth. Tracing her lips, gliding over her teeth and toying with her tongue until her fists clenched his T-shirt and she moved to straddle him. With effort, Alex stopped her with one hand that wanted to tug her closer instead of pushing her away.

"Too much?"

Alex inhaled. "If we go there, I won't be able to stop."

Kate's eyes dropped to the bulge pressing against his cargo shorts. "Right. So we need to stop before that happens?"

Alex laughed sarcastically. "Impossible. You enter a room and that happens."

Kate smiled and reached out her hand. "Maybe I could just—"

"No. I vowed to celibacy and I plan to keep that vow."

"So no orgasms?"

"For me." His eyes flashed. "But just because I have to suffer doesn't mean you have to." His hands trailed up her thighs, still spread on either side of his lap.

"No." Kate stopped him with her hands, then thread her fingers through his. "If you have to be good, then I will be, too. There's no sense making it harder than it should be."

"Kate."

She smiled. "Ah, you can say my name."

He rose up, readying to plant a kiss on her neck. "I can say it often if you'd like. But I want to satisfy you."

"You do." Her gaze hit his, full of emotions they weren't ready to explore. "The last time we tried this, it was all attraction and reaction. Let's slow it down this time. Be friends . . . who kiss." She grinned. "But nothing more."

"And you're okay with that?"

Kate peered beyond him, and he watched her for several moments in silence as she thought about it. "For now I am. If I change my mind and I need more, I'll let you know."

"I won't like seeing you with someone else, but if you need that, then okay. Date. Do whatever."

"Will you be dating?"

Alex gripped her hips and focused on her, taking in every inch of her face. God, she was so beautiful. "No."

Her lips twitched, and he knew she was fighting to rein in her excitement. Like him. "All right. Then neither will I."

"You don't have to do that."

"I know."

"Come here." He tugged her to him, pressing his lips to hers; then realizing his lower half hadn't yet recovered from their earlier make-out session, he pulled away before he caused himself anymore pain.

"One thing?"

Worry crossed her face. "Okay?"

"We keep this between us. Trip won't understand. My history isn't exactly noble. He won't trust that we're keeping this innocent. He already told me to stay away from you. Sex or not, he won't like this."

"He's not my father. Or even my brother. Trip has no say-so in who I care about."

Alex smiled. "You care about me, huh?"

"More than I should, based on that cocky grin on your face. But Emery's my best friend. I don't know how I'll keep it from her."

"I don't want you to lie, but we don't have to tell them either."

He could tell of everything they discussed, this was the thing she struggled with the most. She and Emery were practically sisters. And he didn't want to jeopardize their friendship because of his relationship with his brother. He would deal with Trip if the time came. For now, it would be easier if no one knew. Wait until the mares foaled and they saw the success of his matches. Or failures. But he tried to push aside negative thinking.

"I won't tell you what to do," he said. "But if it doesn't come up, I won't be sorry either."

"I can't lie to her."

"Then don't."

Kate chewed at her bottom lip. "But if she doesn't ask . . ."

"Then no harm?"

"No harm."

Relief washed through Alex as Kate settled against him, cuddling up as they watched the end of the game. Was it possible to have his cake and eat it too? He sure hoped so, because this situation walked the dangerous line he'd lived for so many years. But this time, it wasn't his life he was risking—it was his heart.

Chapter Eleven

Kate knocked on her parents' door, eager to see them after a few weeks now of missing each other. Some considered it strange that she still hung around her family so often, but the Littletons had always been a supportive, close bunch. They made it a ritual to have brunch every Sunday and Kate had missed the last two. One because of a dress fitting appointment with Emery and the other a meeting about the school play.

"Katie-bug," her dad called as he opened the door. "Why are you knocking?"

"Um, because the last time I didn't knock I was scarred for life." Kate tried to shake the image of her parents in the kitchen, on the table, doing things she liked to pretend people over a certain age didn't do. Her parents had always been a loving couple, and in truth, she hoped she and her husband would still long for each other after thirty-plus years married, the way her parents did. Still, she didn't want to see it.

"Right," her dad said, not altogether embarrassed. "Well, come on in. Zac's out back with Carrie-Anne. She'll be excited to see you. Charlie and Brady will be here soon."

The smell of French toast and eggs hit her nose, and immediately, Kate thought of fond memories of running around their two-story farmhouse, her brothers chasing her because while they were all older, she was always faster. She loved coming home, loved watching her parents together. And truthfully, they were the reason she craved love and commitment so much. She wanted what they had, wanted to go to sleep with the same person every night and know he would be there for her through the thick and the thin.

But not just any someone.

She used to picture her life, used to think through her wedding and her first real house and kids, the whole future thing, and the man beside her had always been a faceless person, every part of him a mystery. But now when those fantasies crept into her mind, she saw a particular person, and it scared the crap out of her. Alex made it perfectly clear that his focus was on his career right now. That he wanted her to wait. But for how long? Six months? A year? Five years? And what if she waited only to have him change his mind?

Kate had never been the worrisome sort, but she'd also never been in a relationship with someone that couldn't be classified as a relationship. That she couldn't speak about to her best friend. Could she even tell her family? The whole thing left her feeling on edge, like any second she'd tumble over the side and lose all grasp she had on her reality.

The thought made her want to call Alex and cancel their plans for that night, cancel their agreement. But then she stepped out the back sliding glass door and Carrie-Ann ran up to her, smiling wide, and suddenly all Kate could think about was that maybe going slow wasn't such a bad thing.

Zac had married Carrie-Ann's mom within six months of meeting her. She was pregnant a year later, and then just after Carrie-Anne turned four, she left Zac for her gynecologist. Not even joking.

The whole thing made Kate question her disillusioned fairy-tale mentality on love. Her parents' relationship had always been so strong that it had jaded her thinking.

"Hey, you," Kate said, hugging her niece tight.

"You missed the last two weeks." The little girl had inherited her mother's olive complexion and dark hair. If not for her blue eyes, she would look nothing at all like her father, who could be Kate's twin.

"I'm sorry. Won't happen again." Kate kissed the girl's cheek, which earned her a giggle.

"Promise?"

"Promise."

"Carrie, come in and wash your hands," Kate's mom called from the window in the kitchen. Kate waved to her, then glanced down at her niece.

"Better do as she says."

"You just got here. Can't we play for a while first?"

"After."

Carrie-Ann started to protest just as Zac came over and gave her that daddy look that meant do as you're told, and she scurried on into the house.

Zac and Kate sat down at the table on the patio and stared out over the grassy backyard. Their father's garden had grown larger, the landscaping as immaculate as always. The rest of the farm spread out to the west of the house, and though her dad liked to stay apprised of the comings and goings on the farm, he'd long since passed responsibility for actually running the day-to-day operations to her brothers.

Charlie and Brady came out the back door then and sat down with Kate and Zac.

"Heard you went out with Matt," Charlie said, his dark hair gelled in a spiky mess, his jaw as scruffy as ever. "Is that still a thing?"

Kate shook her head. "No. He's a mailman."

Brady smirked, his look clean-cut compared to Charlie. All buzzed light brown hair and smooth shave. "Did you think that would change before the date or something?"

"No, I guess not."

Charlie and Brady disappeared back inside to help carry out food, and Zac turned to his sister. "Then why did you go out with him?"

Kate sighed. "I think I wanted to see. Maybe we'd have amazing chemistry, and I wouldn't care about the rest. Don't you ever do that?"

"All the time," Zac said. "I try to keep dating to a minimum, and I never introduce any of them to Carrie. But when I do go out, I'm always hoping I'll feel something like I did before."

Kate's gaze cut over to her brother and her heart clenched tight for him. "Like with Amy."

He nodded once. "Sometimes I think I'll never trust anyone enough to know the difference."

Reaching over, Kate patted his hand. They'd always been able to talk like this, open and honest, nothing held back. If there was anyone she could tell about Alex, it was Zac.

"I think the right person will make you forget Amy altogether. The right person makes you consider a lot of things you never would before, tests you in the best ways. You'll know it when you find her."

"You talk like you've found a right person of your own."

He focused on her, and Kate drew a breath, ready to tell him, but then she thought about Emery and what she would say if everyone else knew but her, and her mouth closed. "No. Just hoping someday."

"I hope you find someone someday, too. You deserve it."

Kate smiled at her brother as she pushed aside a surge of unexpected emotion. She did deserve someone.

Now, if she could just convince herself to be patient and wait for the person she believed could be the right someone . . . Time would tell, like everything else. But she liked the idea of holding hands with Alex year after year, laughing at his cute humor and exploring the world with him at her side. Maybe it was a fantasy, maybe they would never survive this year, but she'd never know if she didn't try.

Donna Littleton arrived at the table then with plates and a swift kiss to Kate's cheek. "You missed two weekends in a row."

Kate smiled, despite her desire to explain to her family that she worked and was helping plan her best friend's wedding. Occasionally, one of those things would interfere with her weekend life. But she'd learned long ago that explaining these sorts of things never changed her parents' opinions. They had always been family first, anything else second, and she was, too, really. So instead of arguing, she said, "I promise no more missed weekends unless I'm in the hospital or falling over sick or—"

"On a date," her mother finished for her. "You're allowed to miss if you have a date."

Kate looked at her mother. "A date. At eleven in the morning on a Sunday? Trust me when I say that if a man has me on a date at that date and time, he's not likely to get a second."

"I'm just saying that if you need to spend time with a special boy, we'll understand. In fact, I think we can all agree that we would more than support it."

"Support what?" her dad asked as he helped Carrie into a chair, then took the one across from Kate, Charlie and Brady falling in behind him around the table.

"Kate dating."

"Ah, yes. How is your dating?"

Kate felt her face flush. "Everyone at this table besides Carrie has now asked about my dating life. What's going on?" She stared down each of her family members, but it was her mother who spoke.

"We just think it's time for you to date someone seriously. It's been a while and time isn't exactly a friend, if you know what I mean."

Folding her napkin into her lap to keep her hands from shaking, Kate peered up, wishing there could be a text sent to you when you were on the way to an ambush like this: **Warning: attack underway. Prepare your best defenses.**

"I date."

"Your longest relationship was three years ago and lasted six months. I can't even remember his name."

"Vince."

Donna snapped her fingers. "Yes, Vince. What happened to him?"

"He joined the clergy."

Her mother's gaze held on hers. "You're saying he became a monk or something?"

"I really don't know, Mom. Maybe. He decided his passion was for the church."

Eyes still wide, she focused on her plate.

"What?"

"Nothing."

"I've dated others, though. And I just went out with Matt Bridges last week."

Donna set down her fork and stared pointedly at her daughter. "Charlie's friend? The mailman?"

She wanted to scream that she was seeing someone now. Someone with a real job and plans, who could take care of her someday and she could take care of him. Only she couldn't tell them any of that; not the future part because she didn't know if there would be one, and not the present part because no one was allowed to know.

Frustrated, Kate stacked her plate with French toast, four slices tall, then slathered on more butter than should be legal, and covered it all in maple syrup. Only when she cut into the breakfast and lifted a gigantic bite to her mouth did she notice that they were all watching her.

"What?" she asked around a mouthful of food; then her fork dripped syrup onto her dress and she fumbled for her napkin, dropping it onto the patio before she managed to sit back straight, the napkin now covered in dirt, her dress drizzled in syrup, and, by the looks on their faces, her own face very likely covered in some mixture of powdered sugar or syrup or God knew what.

Her brothers all broke into laughter. "Well," Charlie said with a wink at his sister, "at least we know why she can't get a boyfriend."

Chapter Twelve

Alex opened his front door even before Kate could knock and took her hand, closing the door back behind him as he led her back down the walkway.

"Wait, where are we going?" Kate asked, clearly confused. "I thought we were watching a movie."

"We are. But not here."

He opened his garage, walked over to his Harley, and handed her a helmet before fixing his into place.

"Um, what's that?"

"A helmet. You put it on your head. Like so." He pointed to his helmet and Kate rolled her eyes.

"I know what it is, funny man. I mean what am I supposed to do with it?"

Alex cocked his head, another sarcastic reply on the tip of his tongue. "Do you really want me to answer that?"

"I've never ridden a motorcycle. Surely there are practice sessions or something, right?"

He fought the urge to laugh at the clear fear on her face. Damn, she was cute. "How about if I agree to go slow?"

"Uh, clearly you're forgetting that I've ridden with you in that thing." She motioned to his Corvette. "Not sure you know the word slow."

"All right. Point taken. But I won't let anything happen to you. Trust me." He reached for the helmet and placed it on her head, fixing the strap in place, then straddled the bike, peering over his shoulder at her. "Wrap your arms around my waist."

"I'm scared."

"I know. But sometimes we have to play through the fear. Isn't that what we're doing?"

Kate drew a breath and then, with clear reluctance, slipped in behind him, her arms at his waist, sending a surge of heat through him from her touch to every nerve ending in his body.

"You'll keep me safe?"

"I'll never let anything happen to you."

"All right."

"Ready?"

"As I'll ever be."

He backed the bike out of his garage, then took off, faster than he should, but he knew Kate well enough now to know that she needed to conquer the fear first before she could relax. A scream hit his ears, followed by lots of name-calling; then, finally, a giggle of excitement, and the next time she screamed out, he knew she was having fun.

They continued out of Hamilton Stables and onto the main road, and Alex contemplated driving around all night, just so he could hear that sweet scream and feel her pressed against him. Never in his life had one person impacted him so fully, changed his mood with one smile, challenged him to be better. More. He never wanted to let her go.

But he'd promised her a movie, and there were no movies like this. He pulled left down another dark back road and Kate shook against him.

"What is it?" he called as they slowed.

"Nothing."

"Are you afraid?"

"Yes."

"Should I stop?"

"If you stop here, I'll never speak to you again."

Alex laughed. "Then what's the problem?"

"Haven't you ever watched a horror movie in your life? Serial killers live in dark woods. Men with hockey masks or chainsaws, ready to eat your flesh." She shook again, and he couldn't help it. He burst out laughing, the effort to fight it causing him to laugh all the more.

Kate lightly hit his back. "Hey. It's not funny."

"No. You're right. It's hilarious." He laughed louder and sped up, no longer worrying over the evening. This was where he wanted to be, with the person he wanted to be with.

He parked beside several cars in a concrete pad beside an old airport, and Kate slipped off the bike, him after her.

"Where are we?"

"The library sponsors outdoor movies in the field beside the old airport every third Saturday of the month. They rent blankets and you can buy popcorn and everything. All to raise money for a remodeling. I was hoping we could hang out here tonight."

Kate's face lit up and she rose onto her toes, wrapping her arms around him as she pressed her lips to his, but as soon as he tasted her mouth, the hint of strawberry from lip balm or something, he couldn't control himself. He pulled her close, kissing her like he needed her to exist, to keep from floating away. Finally, they broke away and she smiled again.

"This is amazing."

"Yeah . . . it is." Alex threaded his fingers through her hair and kissed her again before forcing himself to pull away. "Come on, it's about to begin."

"What are we seeing?"

"It's a surprise."

Mayor Phillips sat with Penny Salter at a foldout table just beyond the parking, a sign taped to the front that read: MOVIE ON THE LAWN $2 per person, $5 per blanket, $1 popcorn and water.

"Hey there, Mayor," Alex said, greeting them. "Busy night?"

"This one's always a popular one." He motioned out to the field, where, sure enough, a crowd had already shown up, many of the spots in front of the giant screen filled. "What are you having?"

"Two tickets, plus a blanket, two waters, and a popcorn."

Alex passed over the money and Penny handed them the waters, a navy fleece blanket, and a bag of popcorn. "Thank you."

"Have fun."

Alex spread out the blanket in the back and center of the screen, hoping they could get a little privacy this far away. The night was amazingly clear, the stars bright, like they, too, hoped to watch the showing.

Kate reached over for a piece of popcorn as they sat down, and Alex jerked it away. "Hey, hey. This is my bag. Go get your own."

At Kate's surprised expression, he broke into laughter. "Joking."

"Not funny," Kate said, snatching the bag and digging in, which made Alex smile still more. "I don't joke about food."

"Clearly. Am I going to get any of that or . . ."

Kate dove in again, then shoved it in her mouth. "Maybe before, but no way now."

"I see how it is, but little did you know that I'm quick." He tried to grab the bag, and she jumped away. "Oh, you've done it now." He grabbed her legs and held her down, still reaching for the bag, leaving him no choice but to lean over her to try to grab it. And that was when he glanced down, his heartbeat picking up speed at their closeness, her lying flat on her back, his upper body hovering over her. Two inches, three, and their lips would meet.

"I'm going to kiss you now."

"We're in front of everyone."

"We're in front of no one." Then, unable to delay another second, he bent his elbows, edging closer until his lips grazed hers. "Tell me to stop and I will."

"I can't."

He touched her lips, intending to kiss her sweetly, but he could no sooner control the kiss than he could prevent the wind from blowing. Suddenly, his body was flush against hers, all evidence that showed just how much he was enjoying the kiss pressing against his shorts and likely her thigh.

Finally, the sound of the movie beginning broke the trance and he pulled away, distancing himself from her, until she took his hand. "No, you have to sit here," she said, patting the space directly beside her.

"I don't know if I can keep from doing that again if I'm that close to you."

"Good. I want you to."

He laughed. "You're trouble, you know that? Everyone thinks you're so good, but you've just got them fooled."

"Not you."

Alex leaned in and pressed a kiss to her neck, gliding his nose over her jaw. "No. Not me."

Then the movie started and Kate's gaze fixed on the screen. "It's *Steel Magnolias*."

"You told me you liked it."

Her gaze hit his. "That was nearly two years ago, one of the first times we went out."

"What can I say? I pay attention."

A strange look crossed her face, and Alex was wondering if she was upset when she climbed into his lap and pressed her lips to his again. "You continue to blow my mind."

"Hang around me long enough and that'll change. You'll get tired of me."

"I don't think so. I could spend a lifetime around you and not grow tired."

Alex's heart warmed and he pulled her flush against him as they leaned back to watch the movie, his thoughts on the word *lifetime* and how very much he liked the sound of it.

Chapter Thirteen

Kate fought the zipper on her bridesmaid's dress, curious if Emery intended on her going on some insane diet or if she'd grabbed the wrong size, because there was no getting her curves into this dress.

With the dress still on but unzipped down the back, she stepped out of the dressing room and rounded the corner to the three-way mirror, where Emery was sitting. "Um, this thing ain't happening. I need a six, not a four, or a giant tub of—" Her words cut short at the sight of Judith Marian sitting beside Emery, gawking at her engagement ring.

"Honey, you would drop right to the bottom of the Cherokee," Judith said, that fake smile she wore around like a brand-new outfit on her face. Judith had graduated high school with Emery and Kate, but where she had been all cheerleading/popular/class president, Emery and Kate were . . . well, not.

"Kate, there you are," Emery said, pleading with her eyes for a rescue. "We were just talking about you."

"Hey there, Katie."

"Kate."

"Right." Judith beamed. "Can you believe our Emery snagged a Hamilton? Are you as jealous as I am? Because I'm thinking I need to hang out around Triple Run a bit more. See if I can't land one of those brothers."

Kate's teeth ground together. "I'm sure they're both in relationships. Right, Em?"

Emery opened her mouth, but Judith cut in, reminding Kate of reason one hundred why she'd never liked her. "Maybe that middle one, but the young one? He's a flyboy, they say, all over town. May Brinkwood was with him just last month, I heard. Then Carlie Lyston early last year. They say he's been with all of Triple Run and half of Crestler's Key!"

Kate feared her teeth would chip from the effort to keep from screaming at the lady, but then Emery stood up. "So you've been with him, too?"

Judith stammered. "Well, no."

"Ah." Emery nodded. "Guess he hasn't been with everyone after all. And I'd appreciate you not spreading rumors like that about my brother-in-law. Now, if you don't mind, we have dresses to try on."

Emery set off for the dressing rooms and Kate whipped around to follow, her head high despite her dress being unzipped and half her ass hanging out.

"God, what a witch," Emery said as they reached the dressing rooms. "Are you okay? I know you liked him. Or maybe you're over that?" She studied Kate, and once again, Kate felt like crap for not being able to confess that not only did she like him but she was well on her way to another L word. But then she remembered her conversation with Alex, how he didn't want Trip to know, and before she could think better of it, the lie rolled off her tongue.

"I'm over it. Going out with Chris Dickens again, actually."

Emery's eyebrows threaded. "Are you joking? You said he kissed like a lizard."

Kate stumbled as she stepped out of her dress, narrowly ripping it. "Oh, right. Well, he's learned how to be . . . better. Yes, much better."

"So you're dating Chris now?"

"Just one date really."

"And you're over Alex?"

"Last week's news. We're just friends now."

Emery continued to stare at her, then finally nodded slowly, like she wasn't one hundred percent sure. Maybe Kate's face didn't match her words. She'd have to be more careful if she was going to keep up the lie. Lie. A sick feeling worked through her stomach. How was she lying to her best friend?

"Kate?"

"Yeah?" She peered at Emery through the mirror in the fitting room.

"You know you can talk to me about stuff right?"

"Definitely."

She drew a breath, then eyed the dress, like she needed a moment before addressing Kate again. Dammit, why did she lie? She could have gotten out of this without lying. She could have said—what exactly? Anything she said would reveal too much.

"This isn't the right size." Emery reached for the dress's tag, then Kate. "Six right?"

Kate nodded, her emotions bubbling up. They knew everything about each other, shared all their deepest secrets, and now she was hiding something from her. "Right."

Emery disappeared out of the fitting room to find her the right size, and Kate slumped down into the room's only chair, wishing she'd thought this through better. Wishing she could tell Emery the truth.

Wishing it could all be easier. But something told her with Alex, things might never be easy.

Emery brought the size six dress into the fitting room, then stepped out, a giant smile on her face. "This is the dress. It has to be. I love it!"

"Then we'll make it work."

"You need to love it, too."

"No, only you matter with this one, Em. It's your wedding. Your special day. I'll wear a brown paper bag if that's what you want."

Emery laughed. "Yeah, I'd like to see that. Now hurry, I'm excited." She clapped her hands together and disappeared around the corner. Kate couldn't help but laugh. In all her years knowing Emery, she'd never once seen her clap over a dress. It spoke to just how important this day was to her—just how in love she was with Trip.

The smells of carpet cleaner and too much perfume in the shop suddenly felt overwhelming. How did anyone breathe there? How did they stay in the small store for so long without suffocating?

Kate forced herself to draw a breath, then two, ignoring the voice in the back of her head that said she could have all this, too, if only she'd go for a guy who wasn't putting her aside until his career took off. As soon as the thought hit her, she tried to rationalize it away. Alex wasn't putting her aside. She was right by his side. Last night, in fact. But then, if he came in the store right this second, he wouldn't come up to her, wouldn't show that he was hers. In all likelihood, he would ignore her, ripping out her heart in the process.

Why was she doing this?

"Kate, hurry up. You're supposed to be at your parents' house in half an hour."

Kate pulled on the dress, zipped it up, then took in her reflection. The dress was a beautiful turquoise blue. Gentle and beautiful, sort of like the ocean just before sunset.

"Kate."

"Coming." Pushing out of her fitting room, she stepped up to the three-way mirror so Emery could see, only to realize it wasn't just Emery out there any longer. It was Trip and Nick . . . and Alex.

"Hey, sorry, they were heading to the batting cages, so I asked Trip to stop by to give an opinion on the bridesmaid's dress. Hope that's okay?"

"Of course. It's his wedding, too." But instead of meeting Trip's gaze, her eyes locked on Alex, who was staring at her like she was the best thing he'd ever seen in his life.

"You look amazing," he said, and Kate suspected he'd let the compliment slip, but he didn't try to cover it up. Instead, he continued to watch her as his brother complimented her, too.

"See you later, then," Trip said as he hugged Emery.

"Yeah. I was going to see if Kate could come over to help stuff invites." She turned to Kate, then. "Unless you're going out with Chris again tonight?"

Alex choked, then sputtered. "Come again?"

Emery cocked an eyebrow, then peered back at Kate. "Are you, or do you think you could help?"

"Sure; what time?"

"Five. And no Chris tonight? Too bad. Maybe next weekend."

Kate stared after her real date for next weekend as he disappeared with his brothers out the door, curious how long they would have to pretend. And how long before she became tired of it.

Too soon, she feared.

Chapter Fourteen

Alex quickly texted Kate that he was sorry for being an awkward ass at the dress shop, that he wasn't sure how to act, and waited with bated breath for her reply. He could see the sadness on her face the moment he entered the store with his brothers and did little more than stare at her. Didn't she know that he wanted to go to her? That he wanted to do more than tell her that she looked amazing, that he wanted to show her just how amazing she looked, how amazing she made him feel? But he couldn't. All he could do was offer that small compliment and hope she deciphered the rest from the way he couldn't pull his eyes away from her.

"What's got you so distracted?" Trip asked as they sat down at the Triple Run Diner for lunch.

The smell of bacon and fried foods hit his nose, and though he knew it was the unhealthiest thing on the planet to eat, he didn't care. He'd skipped dinner the night before and had nothing more than coffee that morning. His phone pinged then, with a text from Kate saying no worries, and he released a breath, eager to stuff himself with junk.

"Are you going to answer?"

Alex eyed his brother, then the laminated menu in front of him. "Nothing. I'm starving. I haven't eaten a thing since lunch yesterday." Then, needing to deflect Trip's attention, he added, "What's with Nick these days?" Alex nodded to his brother, who'd stopped outside to take a call. He paced the sidewalk in front of the building, his form appearing and disappearing from view of the diner's wide front windows.

Trip turned around to watch Nick, the two brothers staring with concern at the third, before finally Trip shook his head and switched his attention to his menu. "No idea. He asked if we could meet this afternoon, but he didn't say what it was about. Are you going to be there?"

"No. He didn't say a word to me about it."

The diner was crowded for lunch, so he didn't take offense when Becca swept over to their booth, pad ready, and hurriedly said, "Order."

"Now is that what you call customer service?" Alex joked.

Becca cocked a hip and turned her aggravated brown eyes on Alex, her ponytail swooshing from her tiny head roll. "Now look here, Alex Hamilton, I am in no mood for your little cutenesses. Take that crap elsewhere. There are a thousand people in here and it's a thousand degrees in the back. You're lucky I came over at all and didn't bring you whatever I wanted you to have instead." If Alex hadn't known her since she was little, she and Nick best friends from the moment they could walk, he'd have been intimidated by her spiel. As it sat, he had to fight to keep from laughing.

"Yes, ma'am. Sorry. I'll try to keep my little cutenesses to myself from now on."

"Give it to that pretty red-haired friend of Emery's I keep seeing you with. She's adorable."

Alex's gaze shot to Trip, who had his head tilted in question. "Oh, really? Do tell. When have you seen Alex with Kate?"

Shit. Alex lifted his gaze to Becca, hoping she could sense what he was telling her, that she needed to zip it and fast before Trip unloaded on him in front of half the freaking town.

Becca opened her mouth, but then Nick walked up and her attention fell on him, the creases around her eyes softening, a small smile tempting her mouth, but she seemed to keep it at bay. Hmm, he knew Nick had always harbored feelings for Becca, whether he admitted it or not, but he'd never considered that maybe Becca felt it, too.

"Hey, stranger. We were supposed to see that new *Avengers* movie last week. What happened?"

Nick stared at the table, his breathing heavy. "Sorry, what?"

"Are you okay?" Alex waved over the water girl and handed Nick a glass, but he didn't take a drink. He just continued to look like he was seconds away from a panic attack.

"What happened?" Trip asked, taking on the older brother role.

"Nothing. Let's eat." Nick picked up the menu, but his hands were shaking so badly it fell from his grasp.

"What the hell is going on? Tell us. Now."

"I said nothing. Leave it all right?" Then he stood, narrowly knocking over his water in the process. "Listen, I have a call to make. I have to go." He turned his attention on Trip. "We still on at four?"

Trip nodded. "Sure, but why don't you let us take you home?"

"I'm fine."

"Nick—" Becca started.

"I said I'm fine." Then he walked into a person trying to slip into the booth behind theirs, said a quick apology, and fled from the diner.

"What was that?"

"First the funeral home, now this?" Becca said.

Trip and Alex both looked at her. "What do you mean, the funeral home?"

"I was driving by Dawson's yesterday, saw him come out and squat down on the front steps, his head in his hands. I tried to get his attention, but the light turned, and it looked like he didn't want company. Tried to call later that day, but he didn't answer. Actually, he rarely answers when I call these days." Someone waved for Becca to come over, and she apologized before leaving them alone.

"What would Nick be doing at a funeral home?" Alex asked, his eyes looking out the diner window as though he'd find the answer there.

"I don't know," Trip said, "but I'll find out this afternoon. Something's not right, and it's time he told us what the hell's going on. I'll tell him to meet us at the conference room at four."

"Us?" Alex asked.

"Yes. Something tells me this concerns all three of us, and he's going to tell us. Today. Whether he likes it or not."

Kate passed out the craft project she'd prepared for her students, a smile on her face despite the disaster that was sure to ensue. Alex's text had been sweet, and though she didn't like that they were hiding their relationship, she was pleased that he cared enough to apologize. That he knew how hard this was for her. She had a feeling she wouldn't be able to keep this going for long, and his understanding would make it all that much easier for her to discuss her feelings with him.

"What are we doing with these?" Greer asked as he waved the paper fan in front of him.

"We're decorating them," Kate said with another smile. Or maybe she'd never stopped smiling. Gah, she was so gone. Unbelievably and totally gone. "I thought it would be fun to pass out fans at the play. Everyone here has five white paper fans. You can decorate them however you like. We'll have the greeters at the auditorium's doors hand them out as people enter."

"What if we don't make enough?" Suzy asked. "What if someone doesn't get one?" And here was one of the many reasons Kate adored Suzy. Her heart was bigger than all of Kentucky.

"It'll be fine. Likely we'll have enough, but if we run out, then we do. No one will mind, I promise. Now, I've picked up lots of different things for decorating and I'll sit them all up here." She set out the baskets of glue and scissors. Sequins and stickers. Paint pens and glitter. Plus a basket of odds-and-ends things like tiny plastic bugs, which she felt sure the boys would love. "You can quietly come one by one to get whatever you would like, then go back to your seat. Once you're done, set your fans on the back table to dry. Jake, you can start," she said, pointing to the boy at the front of the right-hand row.

He walked up, grabbed the things he wanted, and went back to his seat. Then, one-by-one, each student came up to collect goodies for decorating. Kate beamed at her class. She was going to miss them dearly. Beyond the one bloody nose incident, it had been an easy and enjoyable year, with no one causing any major issues at all. She knew she wouldn't be so lucky every year and tried to take a moment to appreciate the class. Her gaze scanned the walls, the art the students had worked on the week before about the play, and that was when her gaze landed on one of the drawings, a picture of a stick figure with red hair and a stick figure with blond hair, the words, *Ms. Littleton aka Juliet* spelled out below the red-haired figure and *Alex aka Romeo* below the blond. She couldn't help but smile. She'd tried to keep their flirting to a minimum around the kids, but she'd learned a long time ago that kids saw and heard everything. They were so much smarter than adults.

Just then, she heard a tap at her door and walked quietly over, peering out the glass, and her soft smile took over her face. "Continue working. I'll be just outside." She eyed the class for a moment, but they were working away on their fans, and her pride in her class soared. Stepping out, she closed the door quietly and spun around.

"What are you doing here?"

Alex peered down the hallway, then took her hands and pulled her to him, kissing her lips once, then twice, like once would never be enough. She grinned, feeling all too much like a love-sick school girl, but she couldn't help it. She was.

"I needed a little relief from my family and was in the area, so I picked up the signs for the play. Thought you'd like to see them."

He held up the foam-core posters he'd had made for outside the auditorium doors and her hands clenched. Deep purple background and swirling, glittery text read: "*Romeo & Juliet,* A Third Grade Production." Tiny flowers framed the text. She beamed up at him. "You're amazing, you know that? Absolutely amazing. I—" She stopped herself before her emotions got away from her. They weren't ready for confessions of any kind, certainly not ones that began with *I.*

He studied her, his eyes sparkling as though he knew just what she was going to say and wanted to tempt it out of her. "You what?"

"Nothing."

"Uh-huh. Well, I hope it's okay that I came. I thought the class would like to see them."

"I'm beside myself really. Thank you so much." She rose onto her toes to kiss him again, just as she heard shuffling by the door, and her gaze darted over to find several little faces at the tiny rectangular glass, grinning from ear to ear.

Kate opened the door. "What are you doing?" she asked, hands on her hips at the crowd of little girls, but they weren't looking at her. They were looking at Alex.

"We wanted to see your boyfriend again. Hi, Mr. Alex," Maggie said, her cheeks rosy red from embarrassment.

"Hi, Maggie," he said.

"Are you Ms. Littleton's Romeo?"

"Suzy!" Kate went to cover Suzy's mouth with her hand and shoo the girls away when Alex grinned over at her.

"Yeah . . . I think I am."

He kissed Kate's cheek, which resulted in a surge of long sighs from the girls.

"All right, all right. Everyone back to their seats," Kate said, sure her cheeks were as red as Maggie's by now.

Reluctantly, the girls took their seats, and she nodded for Alex to step back outside. "They'll never recover from this, you know."

"What?"

"You. You're a little addictive. Their hearts might never recover."

He leaned into her. "Theirs . . . or yours?"

Kate drew a breath. "Both."

"Well, with yours, I hope it doesn't." He kissed her once, then pulled away. "Got a meeting with my brothers, but want to meet for dinner tonight?"

"I'll be there."

And maybe then they could talk about ending the secrecy around their family and friends, before it caused the spark between them to fizzle instead of burn.

Chapter Fifteen

Alex slipped into the conference room and closed the door behind him. The scent of lemon wood cleaner hit his nose, like always, the familiarity of it somehow comforting. Still, he was on edge.

Even after more than a year of him arriving before everyone else, his heart refused to slow down as he entered that room. The intimidation was too great. The need to impress his father too much. Carter Hamilton was a lot of things—a successful businessman, a loving husband, and a supportive father. To two of his sons. Alex was another story. Or maybe in his effort to find himself, he'd tapped out his father's support. Blaming himself felt a little better than accepting the truth—he would never live up to his brothers in his father's eyes. But he planned to continue to work until his family saw him as their equal.

Drawing a breath, he peered around the quiet conference room. The large oval table shined so bright it looked like someone had painted on the glow. Clearly, the lemon cleaner worked its magic. Behind the table was a large bookshelf full of trophies and awards and recognitions, most with either Hamilton Stables engraved on it or Trip's name.

He remembered when Trip had told them he wanted to become a trainer, how ridiculous it sounded, how Carter all but told him no, and Trip said he'd do whatever the hell he wanted. Carter could be a part of it or Trip would buy his own farm. It was the first time one of them had stood up to their father, and it hadn't gone well at all.

Thankfully, their mother had stepped in, soothed Carter and pressed a hand to Trip's cheek; then she said he could do whatever he wanted, as long as he did what he loved. If he did what he loved, he would always be happy. It was something she'd said to all of them from the moment they were old enough to hear it. Trip had listened, and now he was the best.

Alex was walking that same path, different but the same. Going against the expectation of their father, though maybe with Alex, he had no expectations left and anything would be a step up.

"What are you doing?"

Alex turned from where he stood in front of the bookshelf to find Nick inside the door, watching him.

"Just reading through some of the awards. Are you all right?"

"Yeah, why?" Nick sat down. Though he made an effort to appear at ease, he looked tired. Stressed. Like he hadn't slept in days, maybe even weeks.

Alex took his seat at the table. "You know why. What happened at the diner? Every time I see you these days, you're acting weird, deflecting questions. And then Becca told us she saw you at Dawson's."

Nick jerked up. "She shouldn't have told you that."

"Shouldn't have told us? What the hell does that mean? And why weren't you the one to tell us? What were you doing at the funeral home?"

Nick stared at the wall behind Alex, refusing to meet his stare. "You'll know soon enough. But before they get here, have you already sealed the deal with the McKendricks? Can you change your mind?"

"Why?"

"Trip disagrees with you."

"Isn't the first or last time."

Leaning in, Nick lowered his voice. "Are you sure you want to do this now? Why not take a chance later, when our breeding division is more established?"

Alex laughed sarcastically. "You don't get it, do you? If I don't take risks now, we'll never *be* established. Champions aren't built by matching photos in a book. It's more than that, and I know I've made the best decision for these two horses. That's all I can do."

"Maybe."

Alex's gaze snapped to his brother. "Do you have something to say?"

"Yeah, I guess I do. I think it's possible you're going against him on purpose."

"What?"

Nick huffed loudly. "Don't sit there and act like you don't feel like you're in his shadow. That you don't do things just to test him. You and Trip are polar opposites, but you're both strong-willed as hell. You won't admit he's right and I'm betting he won't admit you are either, so you went with a different match here just so you can rub it in his face if you're right and he's wrong."

Alex crossed his arms over his chest, flexing to keep his anger in check. "Look, I'll admit that I would be proud as all hell if I made the right call here and could say I told you so. But we're family, and this is a family business. His success is mine and vice versa. I would never make this call just to go against Trip. What sort of idiotic bastard do you think I am?"

"The kind who would get involved with Kate though he warned you not to."

Alex straightened up, thrown by the mention of Kate. The conversation had taken a sharp left turn somehow, like Nick was trying, once again, to deflect attention from himself. "That's different."

"So you're saying you aren't in a relationship with her?"

Dammit. "No." But he stuttered, and Nick knew he had him. Alex started to argue again when Nick tossed up a hand.

"I don't want to know. I'm not going to be a liability in this disaster. But I agree with him. She's sweet and you're . . ."

"Not."

Nick shrugged. "We are what we are, brother. I'm just saying maybe you want to think about what's best for her. Not just what's best for you."

"Maybe I'm what's best for her."

"Are you? Because if you're not, then you need to let her go so she can be with someone who is."

Alex had never considered that maybe he wasn't what was best for Kate. He'd straightened himself out, had a solid career with a solid trajectory. Why couldn't he get the girl? Yet Nick's words hit a nerve. "How did you know with Brit?"

Nick pushed back from the table, withdrawing from the conversation. The same way he did every time anyone said his dead fiancée's name. Like the pain, even years later, was too much to bear in his current existence. He had to back away from it. A part of Alex felt bad for reminding him of what he'd lost, but then he thought maybe that sort of pain could never be forgotten. Avoiding talking about it wouldn't make it any easier.

"That I was what was best for her? I didn't. Don't. But I loved her enough to try every day to be that man. Some days I succeeded. Other days I failed miserably."

"I wonder if she would have said that, too. About herself."

Nick drew a long breath and peered up at the ceiling, considering. "Probably. I think living day in and day out with a person is hard work no matter which way you slice it. We all have our tics and vices. The things that no one wants to see that person sees again and again. I think all we can hope for is to find someone whose good times would make us forget the bad and we'd do the same for her."

The air-conditioning clicked on, sending a rush of chilled air into the room. The slight smell of manufactured air hit Alex's nose. He shivered, though he thought that had less to do with the air and its putrid smell and more to do with how Nick's words had hit home.

Alex wished he had the sort of relationship with his brothers in which he could talk out his thoughts and feelings without being judged. But that wasn't their relationship, wasn't him, at least not now. Maybe one day it could be. Though, again, that hinged on his successes with breeding. Still, he liked the idea of Kate beside him, holding his hand through the good and the bad. She made him think clearer, gave him the confidence to make decisions he otherwise might not make, and pushed him to strive to be better. Would he ever meet another woman who would challenge him the way Kate challenged him?

"You think Kate is your person?"

Alex glanced up, each word hitting him square in the chest. Kate, his person. His match. He swallowed. "Yes."

"She's a good person."

"Yes," Alex said again. "So am I."

Nick seemed taken aback by Alex's words, but he didn't argue. Instead, his chin tipped down in a half nod, and he leaned back in his chair. "Well, you always liked taking life-threatening risks."

"What do you mean? Life-threatening?"

Nick smiled. "If you screw it up, hurt her, Trip will hang you. That's if Emery doesn't get to you first."

Alex laughed. "True enough."

Just then, the conference room door opened and Carter walked in, followed by Trip. Their father sat beside Nick, like always, and Trip beside Alex. He expected him to start in on something farm related, but his eyes were on their father. Alex followed his gaze, and noticed he looked considerably paler today, and clammy. And like he'd lost weight. Not fifty pounds or something crazy, but something was definitely off. Then Alex's gaze traveled to Nick to find him staring at the table before him, his eyes clenching tight before reopening. He opened his mouth to ask what was going on, but it was Trip who finally spoke. "How long?"

Carter threaded his hands in front of him and raised his gray eyes to his son. "Two months. Three, if we're lucky."

"Three . . . ?" Alex started, but his words trailed off at the expression on Nick's face. Like he knew something and felt guilty at not having revealed it. Then Trip, who looked like he wanted to vomit. Finally, he focused back on their father, on how frail he looked, and suddenly, he knew. The paperwork Nick had refused to show Alex. The strange behavior at the diner. The visit to Dawson's funeral home. It wasn't all a random coincidence. He was executor on their father's will, which meant . . .

"You're dying?"

Lifting his head a touch higher, like the words had insulted him, Carter said, "Aren't we all? But yes, it seems my time is coming sooner than I'd like."

"Two or three? Are you saying you have two or three months to live? That can't be right. This is a joke," Alex said, glancing between his brothers again. "Say something. Tell me what's going on. Because there's no way he only has two months to live."

"We're only guaranteed this moment and even that's fleeting. Now, to business."

"Business? You just told us you're dying and you want to talk about work? No."

"Alex . . ." Nick said.

"No. I want to know how long you've known. All of you. How long have you known and kept this from me?"

Nick swallowed hard before looking back up. "Six months."

"Six months!" Alex pushed out of his chair, unable to sit there another second with these people who called themselves family yet didn't have the decency to share something like this with him. "You've known for six fucking months?"

"We didn't want to stress you out. You had a—"

"No." Alex pointed at his brother. "You don't get to put this on me. I'm the youngest, but I've been a man for a long time now. And this is not how you treat family."

"Alex . . ."

He felt his world tilting on its axis. All he could think about was how the man who'd taught him everything he knew, who'd pushed him in the best and worst ways, who he respected more than anyone else in the world was no longer going to be a part of his life. And suddenly, he didn't know how to hold that information in, how to make it fit in his brain. Unable to sit there with them another second, he turned for the door.

"Alex . . ." Trip this time, but Alex was long past listening. And long past gone.

Once in his truck, he drove around town, but every place he passed brought on memories of his father. The long stretch of back road where he'd taught him to drive a stick shift. The old snow cone stand where they'd come every weekend during the summer when they were kids. He needed to get out of Triple Run, needed to be around trees and fields and places that didn't remind him of the pain.

And he knew just where to go.

It took a surprisingly short amount of time to arrive at Kate's small house on Rainbow Row in Crestler's Key. A rental, he remembered her telling him, but she had made it her own, and as he walked up the cobblestone path to the front door, he thought he couldn't imagine anyone else living here.

Large hydrangea bushes cradled the front porch, one blue, one pink, and Alex knew Kate would have enjoyed watching them bloom to see which she'd end up with. Past the hydrangeas were three green bushes with the occasional tiny white and yellow flowers. He had no idea what they were called, but the scent reminded him of Kate. Hanging on the front door was a wreath of greens and flowers, fake as far as Alex could tell, and he bet Kate hated that fact. On the front porch was a mat that read "You're Home," and Alex couldn't help thinking *Yeah, I am.*

He knocked on the door and heard Kate call out some expletive, which had him glancing around, curious if he was interrupting something. Please God don't let him be interrupting something. This day didn't need to get any worse.

Then the door swung open, and Kate stood before him, bits of flour in her hair and wearing only a pair of tiny pajama shorts and a tank top. She grabbed his hand and dragged him inside, then glanced both ways out the door before closing it.

"I'm supposed to be sick," she said. "The spring festival's tonight, and normally I volunteer. But I've volunteered every year for five years. It's time some of the others in town step up. I couldn't just say no because I'm a big fat chicken, so instead, I called in sick. Emery's substituting for me."

"Substituting with what exactly?"

"The face painting table."

"Emery? With a bunch of kids?"

Kate cringed. "Do you think she's killed any of them yet?"

Alex's face relaxed so completely at the worry on hers that in two steps he had her in his arms, flour and all.

She stilled, though he felt the rumble through her as she breathed him in, and he found himself doing the same. "I like your smell, too," he told her, which had her trying to pull back.

"Ugh, I'm a mess. I need a shower. I'm caked in cake ingredients. How Patty and Annie-Jean do this, I'll never know."

"What's the cake for?"

She ran a lazy hand over her hair, coating it in more white stuff. "You. The first mare you bred foals today, right? I was going to bring it to your house for our date tonight."

In all the mess with his father, Alex had forgotten. "Um, yeah. I guess she does."

Kate's eyebrows threaded together. "You 'guess she does'?" She studied him, her eyes switching from one of his to the other, searching. "What's wrong?"

Swallowing, Alex peered around for a chair, a couch, something to sit down on before he fell. Now that he was here, the one place he could be weak without judgment, his legs no longer wanted to support him.

"Alex?"

"Can I sit down?'

"Of course." Kate helped him into the small living room, a single couch and a chair angled before a widescreen. A tiny wooden table sat between them, and an area rug underneath pulled the room together. There was a stone fireplace, and on the mantel were photos, most of her family, he supposed, and as his eyes locked on a photo of her and her father, he felt a surge of grief rocket through him, buckling him at the knees, so instead of sitting on the couch, he all but fell.

"Okay. I need you to speak. I'm freaking out here."

He couldn't bring himself to look at her. If he did, he feared he'd break down. "My father is dying."

Chapter Sixteen

Within an hour, Kate had set her and Alex up on her small patio out back, a glass of wine for her and a chilled beer for him, a giant bowl of popcorn on the table. Kate had learned a long time ago that alcohol and popcorn could fix just about anything.

It was late afternoon, the sun not quite setting, but not blazing overhead. The smell of Knock Out roses mixed with the popcorn, and Kate pulled out a chair beside her to prop up her feet. She crossed her ankles and took another sip of wine, then two, knowing she'd work through the glass too quickly if she wasn't careful.

"What pisses me off the most is that they didn't tell me. Nick's known for six months. For six months, and he didn't tell me. I could have spent more time with him. Talked. Enjoyed the little bit of time we have left. But now it feels like time's running out. Two months isn't enough. Not even close to enough."

"Did you ask why they didn't tell you?"

Alex stared at her. "There's no reason not to tell me. There's no justification there."

"I'm not saying there is. I'm just saying they're your family and they're hurting now, too. Maybe it's not the best time to choose to be angry at them."

"I'm not choosing to be angry. I didn't cause this."

Kate turned to him, placing a hand on his forearm to calm him down. "I know that. But see, you're getting angry with me now, too. And I don't think you're mad at me. Or them. I think you're sad."

Inside, she'd allowed him to feel safe enough to talk out his anger. But now they were outside, in the open, where it was harder to hide behind those stronger, childish emotions.

When he didn't respond, she continued. "Is he afraid?"

Alex stopped midway to taking a sip of his beer, tilted his head in thought, then set the bottle back down without drinking. "I don't really know. I didn't ask."

"Well, what *did* you say to him?"

"I didn't say anything. I left."

"Your father tells you he's dying and you bolt without even asking how he's feeling? If he's worried? What you can do?"

"I was—"

"Angry, hurt. I get it. But you're not the one dying. He is. Seems like he's got a lot more room to be angry and hurt than you do."

"They didn't tell me. Like with everything else. I'm the youngest, the one unable to handle responsibility or real life." He pushed out of his seat then, pacing the patio. "I do everything for them. My whole life, I've just tried to find a way to be me and them at the same time, and now, I realize they never saw me as part of them anyway."

Kate stood, too, and eased toward him, wishing he'd sit back down. He was a lot taller than her, which made it hard for her to shove him off that soapbox he'd stepped on. "Look, I know it's nice and warm in that wallowing place you're in right now, but you need to stop and listen to yourself. I don't think they've separated from you. I think you've separated from them."

"I—"

"Just stop and listen for once. You're doing what you love now, right?"

He leaned back on his heels. "Yeah."

"And they're happy with what you're doing?"

"Debatable."

Kate cocked an eyebrow, and he relented. "Fine. Yes. They're happy enough."

"Then why would you feel them not telling you immediately had anything to do with how they see you? Couldn't it be that they knew you had an important decision to make for the McKendricks and they didn't want to add any more to your load? That telling you a week or even a day earlier wouldn't change a thing for him, so why make things harder for you? They told you after you made the hardest decision of your career, to help you. So you didn't have to carry both weights at the same time. I'd call that love. They're your family, Alex. And they need you. Don't bail on them now."

"Kiss me."

Kate jerked to a stop. "What?"

He took a step toward her, reaching for her hand, then returning his hand to his side. Like he wanted the decision to be hers, not his. "Kiss me."

"You don't need to kiss right now. You need to talk out how you're feeling. Do the emotions thing. You need to grieve."

Alex shook his head, taking her hand after all. "No, what I need is you. I felt like shit the moment they told me and left, only to drive around, the weight of it so heavy I wasn't sure how I kept from wrecking. And then I realized only one thing would make it any better—you. All I wanted was to come here, to look at you and have you near me. And now I'm here, and you're saying all the things I need to hear, and all I can think about is how badly I want to feel your lips on mine. So kiss me."

Kate fixed her eyes on Alex, taking in the creases around his eyes, the stress he refused to admit. "No."

His eyebrows lifted. "No?"

"No. I won't be your out with this. You need to talk to your family."

"I don't care about them right now."

"I know. But you will tomorrow."

Alex took another step toward her and threaded his hands with hers, no longer asking. He leaned in closer and drew a breath, releasing it slowly against her cheek. "Kiss me."

The sun had begun its trek down behind the trees, casting a golden and orange glow against her house. In that moment, with the sun setting and the scent of flowers in the air and this man she wanted so desperately before her, begging her to take this further, she nearly relented. God did she ever want to relent. But Kate no longer saw Alex as a fun fling or a friend or some short-term boyfriend. She cared about him, and caring meant doing the right thing.

"Stay for dinner."

"How about I stay the night?"

Kate grinned. "You are such a flirt."

"Only with you."

At that she cocked her eyebrow again.

"All right, fine, but it comes more naturally with you." He leaned in to press his lips to her forehead, and she stepped out of the embrace, wagging a finger at him.

"No, sir. No play until you've worked through this."

"I may never work through this, Kate. I may never be okay with them not telling me."

Kate considered him, then. "Maybe you won't get over it, but you'll do the right thing. I won't let you have regrets here. You can't bring back these moments. You have to force yourself to move beyond your own hurt to help your father through his. Can't you see that?"

"I can. But can't you see that maybe for a day I need to not feel this? Need to not feel like my heart is being ripped out? Can't you just . . ."

He dropped his head to hers, and before he had to say another word, she covered his mouth with hers. "Yes." She ran her hands through his hair and rose onto her toes, the kiss becoming something deeper than they'd ever experienced before. His mouth ravaged hers, with sharp inhales, his breath heaving, and then she felt wetness on his cheeks, and she held him closer, allowing him to lose himself in this moment, in this kiss, in her.

Alex backed her toward the house, refusing to release her from his hold, even as he fumbled for the door. They made it inside, then stumbled as they reached her couch, her crashing down on him as he continued his work exploring her mouth, then her neck and collarbone, pushing aside her tank top so he could trail kisses across her shoulder, then back, forcing a moan to release before she could control it.

"We have to stop."

He ran a hand under her shirt, skimming her stomach, testing the water. "Why? What's wrong with this?"

Kate's heart broke as she peered into his bloodshot eyes. She didn't want to tell him no, not now. Not ever. "Because I don't think you'll be able to stop later, and you made a promise to Trip."

"I don't care what I promised Trip."

Kate cocked her head, studying him. "I know. But you will."

Alex sighed heavily and sat up. "I hate that guy sometimes."

"No, you don't. You love him." Kate ran her hands through his hair, her eyes on his, and she leaned down and kissed him again. "Why don't we go out for dinner?"

"Now?" He ran a hand up her leg, trailing circles around her upper thigh, and she had to bite her lip to keep from moaning.

"Yes, now. Either we leave this house or I can't be held responsible for my actions."

Alex smirked. "Are you trying to say I'm irresistible?" And Kate released a breath of relief at the light that had returned to his eyes. He wasn't over his sadness or anger, but was getting there. One step at a time. He was right, he needed a distraction, but she knew if they continued this, they would end up taking it all the way, and she didn't want him to have regrets with her. If he made the decision to forget what he'd told Trip, then so be it. But right now wasn't the time for that decision, when he was hurt and not thinking clearly.

"You know you are; now get off my couch and take me for a burger, so I can forget all the other cravings I can't have right now."

"A burger?"

"With extra cheese. And fries. Cheese fries. And probably a shake."

"You're going to stuff yourself so you won't think about sex?"

"Damn straight."

Chapter Seventeen

Alex waited while Kate changed into a cotton skirt and a tank top. She'd brushed the junk out of her hair and pulled it back into a ponytail. He wanted to tell her she shouldn't have worried about it—she would be the most beautiful woman there, covered in flour or not—but he knew Kate well enough to realize she cared about what the people in town thought of her.

She shut her door without locking it, causing Alex's brows to lift.

"You're not locking up?"

"Mrs. Daniels has a dog."

Alex glanced over to the house beside hers, where sure enough a large black dog slept away on the porch, ignoring everything around him. "Not sure he's going to run off a burglar."

"This is Crestler's Key." Kate shrugged. "Who's going to steal from me?"

He started to argue that anyone could with the door unlocked when Kate took his hand, and suddenly his words got lost in his throat, and instead he pressed their held hands to his chest as they walked and smiled over at her. "I like this."

She smiled back. "Me too."

They continued on down the sidewalk, crossing over to the square, when the sound of music hit his ears.

"The festival," she said in answer to his raised brows.

"Are you going to get in trouble, then? You're supposed to be sick."

"It's okay. You're more important."

Alex stared at her, but she refused to meet his gaze, and he wondered if she knew that she was important to him, too. So important, in fact, that he found himself completely captivated by her in every way. He wanted to know her thoughts and fears, see her through her tough times, and celebrate the good times. He wanted it all.

They watched as a crowd conjured up before the band, dancing even before they'd consciously decided to join the dance floor. Several concession stands were positioned around the rest of the square— candied apples and funnel cakes and face painting for kids, but in place of Emery was a teenage girl.

"Hmm, Emery must have paid off Mary Elizabeth to cover for her."

Alex laughed. "Probably safer."

They continued on around the square, Alex reaching for her hand, now that they knew Emery wasn't a risk. The sounds of country music followed them from booth to booth, and Alex found himself thinking he could get used to this: the simpler life, a woman he loved beside him.

A few of the restaurants close by had set extra tables outside for customers to enjoy the music while they ate, and Kate stopped at one, her face beaming.

"Let's do Joe's," Kate said, motioning toward the popular burger joint, which was already overrun with people. Briefly, Alex wondered if he should worry about seeing one of his brothers, explaining Kate and why they were holding hands, but then he thought of the meeting earlier and decided he didn't care. They couldn't tell him what he could and couldn't do, and though he'd agreed to the celibacy thing, that didn't include dating.

"Works for me."

Alex held open the door for Kate to go in, and like they were in some episode of *Cheers*, several people called out, "Kate!" She walked away to join a table inside left of the door and Alex followed, wondering again why they weren't still at Kate's house, doing not so very PG-13 things. But as Alex watched Kate move through the crowd, hugging the parents of her students and smiling down at little boys and girls, all he could think was that this was the person for him. This girl. If she stuck by him, he could face whatever.

Including his father's death.

The thought stopped him short, but he told himself Carter wasn't dying today. Or tomorrow. There was time to say the things he needed to say. Now if only he could figure out the words.

Deciding Kate might take a bit longer, he went to the register and ordered two cheeseburgers loaded with fries—cheese for Kate, in case she was serious before—and two beers. He'd get her shake from AJ&P's. No one used sugar the way Annie and Patty used it.

Alex took the table topper and number and the two beers and slipped outside, allowing Kate to visit with her students and their families without him there to rush her. And also because he was eager to get back outside. The afternoon had opened his eyes to two important things. First, his father might drive him to drink, but he was still the only parent he had, and Alex didn't know how to cope without the man who'd taught him to be a man around. And second, he was glad for the celibacy rule. As crazy as it sounded, taking sex out of the equation made him appreciate Kate all the more. They talked, touched, kissed. Slowly, he was figuring out all the spots on her that made her shiver and smile. He never would have learned these things if they were off to one of their beds or couches or tables—all right, not the point. They were taking the time to learn each other, and Alex couldn't get enough.

Smiling, he took a seat at one of the tables outside and leaned back in his chair, grateful the one he'd chosen was away from the lighting, shadowing his expression so he could openly feel all the weight of these things.

"Hey, you disappeared," Kate said, dropping a hand on his chair. He glanced up at her, took the hand, and pressed a kiss to her palm, his eyes never leaving hers. A tiny shiver worked through her, and Alex smiled at finding yet another spot.

"Do you have to sit all the way over there?" He motioned to the chair across from him at the two-chair table.

Kate took the seat, then a pull of her beer, and leaned in. "This little outing is supposed to calm the storm, not egg it on."

"Are you saying you can't even sit beside me without wanting me?" He laughed at the bit of pink rising in her cheeks. "Well, at least it's not just me. Get over here." He gripped the wrought-iron chair and dragged it closer to him.

"You're such a barbarian."

"I want what I want."

Her gaze lifted to his. "And you want me?"

"More than I've wanted anything in a long, long time." He threaded a hand into her hair, allowing those silky curls to slip through his fingers. Then, unable to hold off with her biting her lip like that, he leaned in and pressed a slow, simple kiss to her lips. But then she groaned against his lips and pressed harder, clearly forgetting that half her class was in the restaurant. He pulled away, chuckling. "I'll admit, it's going to be a fun challenge keeping you on the good side." He pressed another kiss to the spot just beside her ear and whispered, "When you so desperately want to be bad."

Kate started to say something, like argue, when the waitress brought their food. They dove in, and Alex appreciated that Kate ate like a person should eat without nibbling at the food to keep her weight in check.

"I'm going to talk to my father. Apologize."

"Good."

"I think I was just too hurt before to hear him out. Not that he really wanted to talk about it. He announced that he had two to three months to live and then immediately asked what was going on with business."

"He probably doesn't want to talk about it. It could make it harder for him."

"Maybe. But then, talking about hard things is part of life."

Kate stilled. "Right."

"Are you all right?"

She toyed with her straw, and Alex reached a hand over to her thigh. "What is it?"

"Nothing." She stood and reached out her hand. "Dance with me?" She nodded toward the dance floor, and Alex hesitated.

"You want to go over there, in plain sight of the world, and press your body against mine while we move slowly? Isn't that a little fuel to the fire, Red?"

She swallowed hard, no hint of humor on her face, and Alex saw a change in her eyes. She was telling him that she wanted to put herself out there, asking him to do the same. But could he do that? Could he openly date Kate? Ignore his brother's concerns and go for it? With one long look in her eyes, the spark between them igniting, his skin buzzing away as though it wanted to be close to her, he stood and threw some cash on the table, then took her hand. "Lead the way."

Early evening had set in, the sun a distant memory, the clouds fading away to the night sky. They walked past street lamps that seemed to pop on as they passed, like even they could feel the energy between Alex and Kate. Then she gripped his hand tighter, and instantly he felt the spark charging, his hand and arm buzzing, until his whole body became a slave to this tiny woman with kindness and personality in spades.

Several heads turned as they passed, and a flicker of possessiveness hit in his chest as he pulled her to him, one hand in his and tucked tight against his chest, the other around her waist. He dipped his head to her hair, drawing a slow breath, and damn if it wasn't like taking a shot of oxygen. His insides came alive, everything else disappearing around them, just Kate in his arms. The dance turned slower, until they were barely moving, and without thinking, his eyes fell shut. The pain of his father's impending death disappeared for a moment, freeing his heart to feel everything in real time, in full weight, and for once he didn't allow it to scare him. How had he, Alex Hamilton, become the kind of man who longed to be with one woman? He didn't know, but one thing he knew for sure: he'd stay as long as she would have him.

Pulling her still closer, he moved the hand he'd been holding around his neck to meet the other and danced, forgetting everything else.

For this moment, the stars appearing above them, Kate was all that mattered.

Kate pushed through her front door, uneasy from her skin to her bones. She and Alex had danced until the band said good night, their bodies connected the entire time, and one thing became apparent with each passing second: she was falling for him. Hard. Not sampling the experience to see if he was a good fit, not trying to pick apart his flaws. She was falling. Head over heels, deep in the water, nothing available to save her from this drowning. And though she knew she should ask him to leave so she could think and process, the thought made her want to latch on to him even tighter.

So instead of doing what she should do, she turned around on her porch, darkness all around them, the door ajar but not yet open, and said, "Stay with me."

He released a breath and took a step toward her, his hands finding her hips. "Kate . . ."

"I know. But I'll be good. I just want you in my bed. I want your smell there once you've gone. I want to wake up to your arms around me."

Alex pressed a kiss to her forehead, and she thought this was it, the moment when he refused her and told her they were moving too fast. He couldn't do a relationship. This had to stay simple and casual and easy. But then he took her hand and led her into her house, shutting the door behind her without a word.

It was late, nearly one now, and she knew he had to be at the barn early. She had been selfish to ask him to stay, but she was never selfish. With anyone. For once, she'd asked for what she wanted and she didn't want to take it back.

"Where's your room?"

"You'll stay?"

"I'll do anything you ask me to do."

Her heart warmed and she took his hand again, leading him back to her room. This was the moment when things would typically elevate, a kiss would turn intense and clothes would come off, but they had rules to follow—clothes on, no sex—so what now? Though Kate had always longed for slower intimacy, she'd never really experienced it and had no idea how to proceed.

But soon her fears were dispelled as Alex, like always, took the situation under his control. He nodded to her bathroom. "Extra toothbrush?"

She smiled. "Extra everything. I like to be prepared." Though now that she thought about it, she didn't have a condom. For today, that shouldn't be a problem, but hopefully one day it would. She'd need to pick up a box.

"After you," Alex said, gesturing to the bathroom. They went in together, brushing their teeth with their eyes connecting more often than not in the mirror. Then he stepped out for her to wash her face and change into her pajamas.

Kate found her reflection in the mirror and mouthed to herself, *What are you doing?* Then, shaking her head, she changed into her normal pajama shorts and tank top, not wanting to tempt either of them with anything too sexy. Still, she sprayed a few spritzes of her favorite body mist onto her skin. After all, smelling good didn't equal sex. It could be innocent. Maybe.

She stepped out to find Alex had pulled off his golf shirt to expose all those muscles and lines she loved from their time together before. She tried to remember if he'd always been quite this perfect, and as his eyes hit hers and he swallowed hard, taking her in as if she lit his insides in the same way he lit hers, she knew he hadn't. Because before there were no feelings involved, no risk of losing her heart. But as she stared at the man in her room, nothing on but a pair of low-hanging cargo shorts, his hair a disheveled mess, and absolute affection in his eyes, she knew her heart was already gone, swallowed up by his kindness and humor and care.

"You can't sleep in that," he said, pointing up and down at her pajamas.

Kate stopped and peered down at her choice of sleepwear. "Why not? I'm at least clothed."

He released a short laugh. "Yeah, no. Those bits of fabric don't count as clothes."

"You don't have a shirt on."

"I can't sleep with a shirt on. Or shorts." He pushed his shorts to the ground, and her gaze dropped down to his navy plaid boxers, barely containing how much he wanted her back.

He groaned and turned away. "That's out of my control. Especially if you keep biting your lip like that."

Kate released her bottom lip, not realizing she'd been biting it. But damn, this man with his deep tan and streaks of blonde hair and endless green eyes that looked at her like they saw her and only her, was her undoing.

"Maybe we should just get in bed."

Kate walked over to the left side of the bed, climbing under the covers, then patted the space beside her. Her room was all floral quilt and flowers on her dresser, a simple painting over her bed. She'd purposefully decorated it to make it a soothing, comforting place to end up every night. But it didn't feel comforting to her right then. Not in the least. Her pulse raced and her skin prickled, and parts of her body were reacting despite her efforts to try to control them.

"You're not wearing a bra."

Her gaze lifted. "I can't sleep in a bra."

Alex nodded, swallowed hard, then nodded again. He ran a hand over his jaw, then through his hair, causing it to spike out in the sexiest way imaginable.

Finally, he seemed to gain some control and went to the right side of the bed and pulled back the covers, and a sharp breath whooshed out of his mouth as his eyes met hers. "Shit." He glanced down and Kate did the same, to see that he'd popped free from his boxers. Just how badly he wanted her was pointing at her now, tempting her to say screw the celibacy thing; she wouldn't tell anyone. The secret was safe with her.

"Maybe I should sleep on the couch."

Blinking hard to force her gaze back up and away from temptation, she reached out for him, guiding him into the bed. "Maybe we can be together without being together."

She pressed a kiss to his chest and he flinched. "Kate . . ."

"Trust me."

Trailing her hand over his pectoral muscles, then abs, then the long contours of his thighs and back up, causing him to groan, she covered his mouth with hers, the kiss intended to slow things down, but he gripped her tightly, his tongue darting inside her mouth, unable to hold back.

"Oh, God," Kate moaned as his hands went to exploring her body, across her backside, up her back, before slipping under her tank top to her breasts. "Stop, before . . ."

"I can't." He tugged her close, lifted her shirt, and ran his tongue over her nipple, then sucked it into his mouth. Kate came undone, the tension and want she'd felt all those weeks springing to the surface, turning off her thoughts and turning on the rest of her.

"God, Alex . . ."

He lay her back and ran his hand down her stomach, cupping her heat as his mouth went back to her breasts, then he dipped inside her shorts and panties, stroking her slick core, and suddenly she couldn't be good any longer. She bucked as he drove a finger inside her, then two, his tongue continuing its delicious exploration of her neck, her lips, back to teasing her nipples, driving her higher and higher, until she couldn't breathe or think or feel anything but him everywhere. Finally, he plunged his fingers inside her once more and she exploded, unable to hold off any longer, her hands clenching the pillow behind her head, as her release continued on and on and on.

Alex slowed his movements, bringing her down. But it took several long breaths, her heart still hammering, before she could glance over at him. "I'm so sorry." Her gaze dropped to his erection, still very erect, and he shook his head.

"I'm not." He leaned down to kiss her sweetly, but soon the kiss deepened and he groaned against her lips. "Better take a shower, though. Is that all right?"

"But why don't I . . ." She moved her hand toward him, but he stilled it.

"No. I'll want more. I just need to cool down." He pushed out of the bed, then closed the door behind him, and Kate felt both absolute elation and absolute guilt. She'd agreed to be good, but she feared there was no being good around Alex. They'd have to talk about this if their relationship was going to continue. Surely he could do certain things without going back on his word. But while the rule frustrated her, she found herself respecting him for keeping it. He might come across as the wild, untamable Hamilton, but deep down he was more. So much more.

Alex reappeared twenty minutes later and crawled into bed with her, pulling her close against him and kissing her cheek. "Good night."

"Are you okay?"

"I am now."

Chapter Eighteen

"No, you need to actually hold her hand, Greer," Kate said, pointing to the little boy they'd selected to play Romeo. A short boy with dark hair and dark brown eyes. He turned his eyes on Juliet, both her character and her actual name, a grimace on his face. "Just her hand." The boy reached out, then retracted it, causing Juliet to frown down at her hand as if it were infected with some rare African disease.

The play was a few weeks away now, and little Romeo could recite his lines like the best of them, but he refused to hold little Juliet's hand, and Kate hadn't even mentioned the kiss on the cheek she hoped to bring them to by the end of rehearsals. Holding hands seemed like the easy part, a slow move in the right direction. Nothing big. But then she thought of holding hands and dancing with Alex a week before, and him spending the night with her, then again before he left for Ireland to talk about a stallion purchase. She had no idea how much she'd miss him until that first night, her bed cold from leaving the A/C on while she went out with Emery for dinner and no Alex to warm her up. Seven days had never felt so long.

"Look, it's easy." Kate walked over and reached down to take Greer's hand, which was a mistake. The other boys began to snicker and point, and Greer turned six shades of red before pulling away. Okay, now what?

He dropped his head and peered up at Kate from below his lashes. "Can I quit, Ms. Littleton?" he whispered. "I can't—"

"No quitting allowed at play practice," a deep voice called from the auditorium doors. Kate's eyes flashed up, a grin spreading across her face. She bit her lip as he took the three steps up to the stage and walked over, focusing on Greer. He still hadn't looked at Kate, and she was dying to see those amazing green eyes trained on her. "It's just like baseball. Do you like baseball?"

Greer nodded, and Kate wondered where he was going with this.

"You practice so you get good at it right? To get comfortable on the field? Same thing. Let me show you." Alex reached a hand out for Kate, his gaze lifting for the first time, and it was like receiving a direct jolt to her heart. Dead and now alive. Butterflies and tingles and sparks swarmed her stomach as he slipped his hand into hers, gaze held. "See, practice. Hi," he said to her with a smile.

She beamed. "Hi."

The girls all *awwed* while the boys looked away like they were witnessing the most disgusting thing on the planet.

Alex released too soon, and Kate fought the urge to pout.

"You try," he said to Greer, who looked over at Juliet again like she'd sprouted horns. At this point little Juliet was on the verge of tears, and Kate had decided to move on to another scene when Alex said, "Go stand over there. I'll fill in for Romeo for now."

"Alex—"

"Shh, you're pulling me out of character," he said to Kate. She smiled again and walked away. "All right."

He bent down to Juliet. "I'm Alex. Okay if I act out this scene with you?"

She grinned brightly, and Kate thought there wasn't a female alive who could resist him.

The class quieted down as Alex and Juliet took center stage, each holding a copy of their lines for the scene, and then Kate felt her body go numb as he started to read, his voice deep and passionate, no hint of joking. He wanted Greer to see that it wasn't embarrassing to take on this role, but as he continued through Romeo's lines, Kate found herself transfixed by him, the words, how he freely offered himself to help others. Her chest burned with emotion and she crossed her arms over it to try to hold it all in for fear he'd see just how much he'd affected her.

When they reached the line where Romeo took Juliet's hand, Alex got down on one knee and reached out, taking Juliet's small hand in his large one, and when Juliet spoke then, so clearly in awe of this man before her, Kate found herself picturing her future with Alex. A white picket fence and him holding his daughter in his arms, nothing but love and adoration on his face. He would be that kind of father, the one who dressed up and acted silly, careless of anything but the giggles of his children. It made her realize that she had no idea where this was going with Alex. Was it just fun? Was it more? She had to know, but asking could result in disappointment, and they'd just begun being whatever they were. Surely she should wait, see how things played out, avoid pushing him.

But as she watched him reply to Juliet, the girl's hand still in his, a warm smile on his face, Kate knew she'd need to have the conversation soon, else her heart might never recover from Alex Hamilton.

They finished the scene, and immediately, Greer took his spot as Romeo, eager to practice again. To get it right. He still looked awkward holding Juliet's hand, barely touching her at all, but it was major progress from where they'd been at the beginning of practice.

Alex settled in the chair beside her to watch and took her hand, his long fingers gliding over her fingers, tickling her palm. "I missed you."

"I missed you, too. So much."

"Are you busy after?"

"Yes," Kate said, continuing to watch her students perform. "Hot date."

Alex jerked back, clearly affected. "Uh, all right. I guess we can get together another—"

"With you."

The smile that took over his face was enough to cause Kate's heart to soar, tingles to work through her. Did he really think there was someone else? That he could be so easily replaced?

"Sorry, I was testing you."

"You're lucky you didn't have to call an ambulance. Pretty sure my heart stopped."

Kate tightened her grip on his hand. "You're cute."

"You're beautiful."

She peered over to find him staring back at her, no hint of humor on his face now.

"How long until practice is over?"

"Right now." Kate clapped her hands to get her students' attention. "We're ending here. Great job."

"We still have five minutes," Juliet said, her dreamy eyes on Greer, and Kate couldn't help but smile. "Is this because your boyfriend's here and you want to go hold hands with him?"

Kate's cheeks burned. "No." *Yes.* "It's just a good place to stop. See everyone next week."

Once the kids had all left the auditorium, Alex walked up behind her on the stage, took her hand, and twirled her around, then brought her in close. "Dance with me."

"Here? There's no music."

"There's always music." He began to hum the country song they'd first danced to last week, and Kate wondered if you could die of happiness.

If your heart could fill and fill until it could no longer take it.

"You make me happy," she confessed, her voice a whisper.

He kissed her head. "So much it scares me."

"I don't want to hide this from Emery anymore. My family."

"Okay."

She lifted her head. "But I thought—"

"I never want you to feel like this isn't real, that you can't say or do whatever you like. I'll handle my family."

"I don't want to cause a problem for you, though."

"You won't."

"I—"

Alex stepped a fraction of a step away from her and lifted her chin so he could peer into her eyes. "You cause a problem? You're the best thing to ever happen to me. I don't know how my life ever worked without you."

"I feel the same way."

His forehead dropped to hers and she closed her eyes, taking him in. "Don't leave me, okay? I kind of like having you around."

"Leave? You couldn't force me away, Red. I'm here to stay."

Kate's heart took off, refusing to come back down, but a voice in her head told her to tread cautiously. Where Alex was concerned, she could just as easily find happiness . . . or despair.

Alex opened the door to his Corvette for Kate, eager to take her on another long drive, to hear her squeals of happiness, and this time kiss her under the sunny day's sky. No worries, just them together.

"Ready for this, Red?"

She grinned. "You were great back there, you know. Amazing actually."

"Which part are we talking about here? I like to think I can act and dance equally well. In fact, I should probably consider a career change. Alex Hamilton, performer."

Kate laughed loudly this time. "Yeah, I don't think so. And I meant with the kids, though your dancing works for me, too."

He shrugged. "Kid needed a little confidence is all."

"I can't believe he kissed her cheek by the end of rehearsal. I thought it'd take me another week or two to get him to that."

Alex smirked. "Now, give the man a little more credit. He was nervous, but he's still a man."

"He's eight."

"A little man but a man all the same. I knew he'd rise to the challenge."

"You're amazing, you know that?"

He leaned in to kiss her lips, his eyes closing as the sweet and spicy taste of cinnamon hit his lips, then his tongue. "You're not so bad yourself." He closed her door and walked around to the driver's side, unable to recall the last time he'd been this happy.

Ireland had proven to be a successful trip, and Hamilton Stables would soon be home to a sire that had the pedigree to produce some amazing offspring. Alex knew the moment he saw the stallion he wanted him, could already see him in one of the stallion stalls, becoming a part of the farm. He arrived back home and then, three calls later, he had some of the racing industry's top owners interested in breeding their mares with the stallion. A little prodding and agreement to a secret discount on the stud fee and suddenly, that stallion was going to be a happy horse in the next few weeks.

Now, if he could just figure out what to do about his father. He'd yet to talk to him about his cancer, unsure of what to say, and Carter had never been an overly emotional man. They'd spoken twice since he'd told him, and both times Alex had tried to bring it up but ended up backing out. How did you tell the strongest man you knew that you were sorry his body had failed him? How did you find the words to convey how much he meant to you?

"What happened to your smile?" Kate asked, reaching a hand up to stroke his jaw. He took the hand in his, kissing it, before releasing to put the car in reverse, then pulled out onto the main road.

"Just thinking."

"How was Ireland?"

"Better than expected. We bought him."

Kate clapped, and his smile returned. He loved how his successes made her so happy. That, he realized, differentiated this one from all his other relationships. Most women he'd been with thought only of his name and money, caring nothing about him or what mattered to him. Kate was the opposite, which made him fall for her all the more.

"Can I see him?" she asked.

"He's not at the farm yet. Set to deliver next week. But I can show you a few new broodmares we have. Plus Trip and Emery are running Craving Wind this afternoon. Want to go watch?"

"I'd love to."

He kissed her hand again and then leaned back, allowing his father to slip into the back of his mind. Maybe he'd find the right words today, call him and confess all his worries and doubts and fears. Maybe.

Before long they were on a different back road, and Alex let the car go, roaring to life, and it reminded him of watching one of their Thoroughbreds launch from the gate, all muscle and speed. He loved every aspect of horse racing and wondered how he'd ever considered doing something else with his life. He loved the horses, loved their farm—loved his family.

His throat constricted as he thought of his mother and now his father leaving them. Had Nick and Trip said their goodbyes? Did you say goodbye to someone who was still living? He tried to think of something else before his grief overwhelmed him, but when he came up with nothing, he did the only other thing he could do to force the thought from his mind. He sped up, faster and faster, until Kate's screams of delight replaced the pain in his chest. They continued down the long stretch of road, turned around, then went back the way they'd come. Then he cut over to another road, this one shadowed by trees, the soft sounds of birds greeting them as he slowed the car, unable to stay away from her another second. He parked beside a large oak tree, the road more grass and dirt than street at this point.

"Come here." He unbuckled her seat belt and tugged her to him, so she sat in his lap.

"What are you doing?"

"Kissing you." He gripped the back of her head and brought her lips down to his, relishing in the feel of them, at the tiny sounds she made as the kiss built from sweet and soft to ferocious and needy. His tongue swept over her lips, teasing, then he trailed kisses down her neck, to her ear and back, before finally stopping to pull away, to look into those blue eyes that seemed to see more than anyone before her had dared. And for a moment he thought he could do this. With her, he could do this. Maybe for the rest of his life.

Reluctantly, he drove to the farm, sure Trip would call if he didn't show soon, and parked at his house before they hopped in his golf cart to head to the broodmare barn.

The day was hot for spring, without a cloud in the sky, and Alex thought if spring turned this hot, summer would be a beast.

Kate stepped out as soon as he parked, her expression intent as she slipped inside the barn. "Which one is new?"

"These two," Alex said, motioning to the stalls on the left. "Sarah Anderson sent them here a week ago."

"May I?"

"Of course."

Kate walked over to the first, a chestnut with a vibrant coat, herself a winner of the Kentucky Oaks two years before, and gripped the bars of the stall, then reached in as the horse came to say hello. "She's pretty."

"Very," Alex agreed.

Then Kate veered over to the next stall, her head cocked as she took in Sarah's other mare—Brambles. Brambles wasn't the looker of the chestnuts, but she made up for it in heart. The horse had endurance in spades, and Alex had high hopes of coupling her with Pirate Pete to see if they couldn't produce a champion.

"Wow. She's driven."

Alex laughed. "You haven't even seen her run. How do you know?"

"Her eyes. She looks bored in here."

He laughed again. "Likely is."

"You'll match her with Pete?"

Alex peered over at her. "Yes. How did you know?"

She shrugged. "Endurance and speed. That's the winning combination right?"

"So they say."

"You're not convinced?"

"No, you need both, but it's a lot more than that. You can match two champions and end up with a horse who does little more than trot around or who's injured early season due to a thousand things. I think we have to make smart decisions, care for the mare and foal well, then be aggressive with training. That's what we're trying to do here—start and finish at Hamilton Stables. A one-stop shop."

"Seems like you're doing a good job."

"Everything's solid right now, but you know how sometimes you can feel something coming? Like you can almost predict it, but you aren't sure what you're waiting for to know how to stop it? I can feel it, and at this point, I'm just hoping we can bounce back from it."

Kate turned from the mare and reached a hand out to him. "But maybe the bad has already happened with your dad."

Alex took her hand and kissed it before dropping it back and staring out of the barn, to the farm. "Maybe. But I don't think so."

"Well, I'm here for you if you need anything. To talk or whatever."

"I have a feeling your whatever could distract me from anything."

She smiled and started toward him, just as Emery and Trip walked into the barn, and Alex jumped away from Kate, his hands in his pockets so quickly you'd have thought they were on fire and he was extinguishing the flame. So much for him being okay with them knowing.

"Hey, brother," he said, wishing his heart would settle down. At this point, people in Crestler's Key could probably feel the beating. "Sister-to-be," he added with a wink, then an uncomfortable laugh.

Trip paused inside the door. "What's your deal?"

"Nothing." Alex peered around, then locked his eyes on Kate, like he was just seeing her for the first time. The hurt in her eyes nearly had him confessing the whole thing. Judgment be damned. But he couldn't bring himself to say the words. "Just showing Kate here the broodmares."

"I can see that." Trip glanced over at Kate with an eyebrow raised, but it was Emery who seemed to sense something more going on.

"When did you get here?" she asked. "I didn't see your car by the main barn."

Kate pushed her hair from her face and started toward Emery, her mouth open to speak when Emery said, "And why is your hair windswept?"

"The golf cart," she and Alex answered at once, which made Emery peer over at Alex, then back at her friend. Damn, he needed to shut the hell up before he made this any harder for Kate.

"The golf cart. So you drove in with . . . ?"

"Alex."

"So your car's at Alex's house."

"Oh, no." Kate glanced nervously at Alex, then at Trip, then at the mares, like they could help her work through the lie, and Alex felt like an ass for asking her to lie to her friend for him. For not taking the hit, admitting everything.

"So where is it?"

Alex stepped in then, before Kate spontaneously combusted from the stress of trying to figure it out. "I was helping with the play again, so I drove her over. Her car is still at the school."

But as he said all this, Emery's eyes held on Kate. She no longer looked curious. She looked sad, like she knew exactly what was going on and couldn't figure out why her friend would keep it from her. Alex started to just tell her everything when Kate walked around him.

"I heard you're running Craving Wind. Can I watch?"

And just like that, Emery's face completely changed, the thrill of racing so deep in her blood that nothing else could compare. No other worry could take center stage.

"Yes, come! Clark took him down to the track. We were on our way there now."

Alex released a slow breath and then winked at Kate as they slipped out of the barn and back into the cart, their secret safe for another day.

Chapter Nineteen

Kate couldn't speak the entire ride down to the track, her mind on Emery's expression as she questioned her, and the look in her eyes that said she knew Kate was lying. She knew the moment Kate opened her mouth that she was lying, and she wanted to see how many lies Kate would tell before she remembered that Emery was her best friend, that she could tell her anything. Only she couldn't tell her this, but why?

The whole thing with Alex and Trip had started because Trip didn't think Alex was serious, but he *was* serious. About breeding and about Kate. So why continue the lie? And hadn't she told him she wanted to stop hiding, that she planned to tell Emery? Hadn't he said okay? But then she thought of the fear on his face as Trip asked what they were doing, and worry set into her mind. Maybe she wasn't as important to him as she'd thought. Then again, Emery meant the world to her, and she'd still kept up the pretense.

It seemed so easy not to tell her before, the whole if-you-say-nothing-at-least-you're-not-lying thing, but now she realized that not sharing this part of her life was worse than lying. She cared for Alex, more than she'd cared for anyone before him, and the one person who would be most excited about this, she couldn't tell.

"You all right?" Alex asked as he parked the cart.

She drew a breath and released. She'd told enough lies for today. "No." Then, without another word, she climbed from the cart and walked down to the track, eager to watch her friend do what she did best. Maybe then she could figure out a way to tell Emery without actually telling her, but even the thought sounded convoluted. Kate was getting a headache and the day wasn't over yet.

The sun beat down on her shoulders as she walked down to meet

Trip, and she cursed herself for not putting on sunscreen or wearing something other than her tank dress. Her freckled skin burned at the thought of sun, but she'd had no idea Alex would be coming by. Though she'd gotten in the habit of putting on a daily sunscreen, her thoughts had been on other things that morning. And that scared the crap out of her. She was becoming invested in Alex, despite his offering little and her telling herself to expect nothing. Still, her heart refused to listen. And now she found herself making plans, hoping, thinking about their future.

"Hey there, Kate," Trip said, smiling at her as she walked up. "You okay?"

She started to say *hey* and *yes*, but then she caught the look in his eyes, the deeper meaning to his question. "I'm great."

He nodded. "I'm glad. Just be careful."

"Of what?" she asked.

He peered back at her, then to Alex, who was walking toward them.

"He's a good person, Trip. A good man. Through and through. And it's about time you, Nick, and Carter start realizing it. He might try and fail, but at least he tries. Eventually, one of these times that trying's going to take him somewhere and you'll wish you'd supported him. You're a family after all, and you need one another. Especially now." She swallowed hard and looked away. *Crap.* Not only had she gone off on him, but she'd all but confessed that she and Alex were together.

Wishing she hadn't said anything, she walked on to the track's railing, her eyes on the starting gate they'd installed six months before, Emery and Craving Wind now inside.

The gate flew open and Craving Wind burst free, gaining speed so quickly it looked as though he were flying instead of running, and Kate thought, *so that's the name.* It fit. Her heart sped up as she watched them, her tiny friend on this magical creature's back. She thought of her fall at the Kentucky Oaks all those years ago, her in the grandstand with Emery's parents, and the sickening feeling that worked through her when her friend didn't get back up. She'd prayed silently, then aloud, begging her to get back up, and in that moment, she'd feared the worst.

Hours later, in the ER, she'd held her friend's hand, her parents allowing her in to see her by saying Kate was her sister. Which wasn't too far from the truth. Days turned into weeks, her visiting every day, and soon Emery healed. Thanks to Trip and her refusal to give up, she got back on a mount, became the great rider she'd been once more.

But now, as Kate watched her, she didn't feel pride. She felt guilt. She loved Emery through and through, so how could she keep this from her? Kate had known for a while now that she loved Alex. The kind of love that was deep and real. The kind of thing you wanted to scream about from the rooftops, but Kate's experience wasn't so romantic.

She peered around her to where Alex stood with Trip, his arms crossed, his eyes shaded behind sunglasses, but still she could feel his stare on her. Immediately, her chest warmed, her insides swirling around and around. Maybe their relationship wasn't out and in the open, but it was romantic. It was real. It had to be.

Emery went for another few runs, then Clark took Craving Wind, and she met them at the top of the hill.

"What do you think?" she asked Trip. "Could he go another year?"

"He's slower than last year, but not by much. We'll give him a go." She rose onto her toes and hugged him, then kissed him, long enough that it had both Alex and Kate looking away.

"What's wrong, Red?" Alex whispered.

"Not here."

He nodded, then turned back to the couple, who were both watching them.

"You were great," Kate said, plastering on a smile. "He's amazing."

Emery smiled, but it didn't quite reach her eyes. "He is. Hey, listen, do you have some time right now? I need to go sample food for the reception. I'd love your opinion."

"Um, sure. Absolutely." She eyed Alex.

"I need to go make a few calls anyway," he said. "Can you get her back to the school?"

Emery winked. "I've got her."

And with that Alex and Trip took off in his golf cart, leaving Kate to face her best friend. "Hey, I thought the sampling appointment was next week."

"It is."

Kate shook her head. "So then, what are we—"

"I know."

Kate's insides froze over, her heart afraid to beat. "Know what?"

"Oh, come on!" Emery threw her hands in the air and walked away, pacing before her friend, the friendliness from before etched with anger. "This is me. How could you not tell me?"

"I might if you would tell me what you're talking about." At this point, Kate had two options: confess or wait it out. This could all be over some wedding cake disaster, and Kate would ruin everything because her guilt was reading too much into everything. "Was the food-tasting appointment moved?"

"No. It's next week. I lied; how does it feel?" Emery stared pointedly at Kate, and in that one stare, Kate saw the truth: she did know. She knew all of it. "I saw you at the festival. Saw you dancing. Saw him kiss you a thousand times. And all that's fine. But what I don't get is why you didn't tell me. You told me you had feelings for him, so why not tell me when you decided to act on them? Did you not trust me enough? Not think I cared? What it is?" Her anger was replaced by hurt, and she blinked hard, causing Kate to feel even worse.

She drew a long breath and released, focusing on her friend fully for the first time. There was no avoiding this now. "I couldn't tell you," she whispered. "He asked me not to."

"And you listened? This is me, Kate. Me. We tell each other everything."

"I know."

"So why not tell me this? And why would he ask you to keep this from me?" She paused, then understanding worked through her face. "Trip. He doesn't want Trip to know."

Kate nodded. "They gave him a hard time about being serious about work, so somehow he agreed to stay clear of any distractions until the breeding division took off."

"But that's not fair. He shouldn't have to stay away from you if he cares about you just so Trip won't say anything. I'll talk to him."

"No, you can't! Trip can't know."

Emery leveled her gaze on Kate's. "Clearly you don't see how you act around each other. Anyone would know. It's obvious when two people are in love."

"Oh, that's not—"

"Are you really going to start this again? I'm your best friend. You should be able to tell me."

Kate drew a slow breath. "Okay."

"You'll tell me?"

"I'll tell you everything."

Emery held open the door to Patty's Place, a pointed stare on her face as she ushered Kate inside. The ride over consisted of several "So, explain—no, wait until we get there" and "But how have you— no, just wait," until Kate was tempted to order Emery to pull over so she could give her a play by play and stop this half conversation. Also, because Kate was very nervous that she wouldn't be able to explain the full details of their relationship at Patty's, within earshot of half the town.

But now, here they were, taking their seat at a bistro table by the window, and suddenly it occurred to Kate that this was where she'd first met Alex. It was the first meeting between Emery and Trip, and Emery had insisted Kate come with her for support.

So they'd driven over to Triple Run but were early, so they'd stopped at Patty's for breakfast, only to have Alex come over and nearly expose the fact that Emery was meeting with a competing farm. Emery had always raced for her father, but after her accident, he'd refused to put her back on a mount. So she'd done the only thing she could— she'd called Trip, the best trainer in the world and the guy she'd fallen for years before as a teen. Little did she know working for him would bring back all those feelings. Now, eighteen months later, she and Trip were planning their wedding and Kate was falling in love with Trip's brother.

The whole thing had a very Hallmark Movie feel about it, but such was love in a small town.

"Okay, talk," Emery said.

"I need to know first that you won't—"

"I won't deliberately tell Trip anything you don't want me to. We're friends. Nothing could change that. But . . ."

"But you won't lie to him either. And I wouldn't want you to." Kate realized it was the very same thing Alex had said to her, yet she'd found herself lying to Emery anyway. "I'm sorry I didn't tell you before."

Emery rested her elbows on the table, her chin in her hand. "Why didn't you? Really? I know the Trip thing, but I don't think that would have been enough to keep you from telling me. Is it the wedding stuff? Have I become a bridezilla that no one wants to be around?"

"No. Not at all." Kate reached across to squeeze her friend's hand, then she stared out into the bakery, to the couples sitting close, to the mothers and daughters enjoying lunch together, to the teen girls huddled around a table, gossiping away. Finally, it occurred to her why she hadn't told Emery. "I didn't want you to judge me."

"What?"

Swallowing, Kate forced herself to press on. "I'm the romantic. The one who wanted to see all the romantic comedies. The one who gushed about wanting a commitment and getting married and having the whole family thing. You know that stuff is important to me, so I thought if I told you that Alex and I were hanging out, nothing serious, you'd tell me I was crazy. To be with him, to . . ."

"Fall for him?"

Kate's shoulders dropped. "Yes."

The smell of warm bread hit her nose, and Patty arrived at their table with fresh banana bread and two cranberry and apple salads. "On the house, honey," she said, winking at Emery. "Annie would skin me if I charged you."

Emery smiled, then stood to give her aunt's best friend and business partner a hug. "Love you, Patty."

"You too, honey bunches. Now get back to talking about that baby Hamilton." She flashed a grin at Kate and winked. "Not the first time that hot thing's been the talk in here. And likely won't be the last. But carry on." She motioned for a teen girl who was pouring tea and water at various tables to bring over drinks to Kate and Emery, then set off back behind the counter.

"Fantastic," Kate said. "Not only does the entire shop think I'm obsessed with Alex but that I'm one of many."

Emery's eyes turned kind. "You know I love you right?" Kate braced herself for what she would say next. "But I think you need to prepare yourself that they could be right. On both accounts. You seem invested in him, and I don't want you to get hurt if he . . ." She trailed off and cocked her head, shrugging a bit.

"If he bails." Kate took a sip, then two, of the tea the girl brought over, her mind and heart at war with each other. Emery and Patty and the entire bakery full of people were right: Alex was wild and easily bored and tended to act first, think later. But they weren't the ones dancing with him for hours, listening to him whisper sweet words in their ears, holding them close and pressing kisses to them because he seemed unable to stay away. They didn't see him the way she saw him, and it was her relationship and her heart. She might never survive this heartbreak, but wasn't it better to take a chance on someone you loved than live a passionless life?

"He might," Kate said finally. "He might decide he doesn't have it in him to stay. He might decide I'm not the girl for him. But he also might be the best thing to ever happen to me, and I'm willing to take a chance on that. I can't go back to good enough when I've experienced amazing."

"You love him."

Kate bit her lip. She'd yet to say those words out loud and she didn't know how to say them now.

"Kate?"

"Yes. I love him. I love him so much it scares me. I feel lost and empty when he's away and so full of complete happiness when his arms are around me that I want to beg him to never let me go."

Emery smiled at her friend. "Does he know?"

"No."

"Are you going to tell him?"

Kate allowed her gaze to drift out the window, to a couple walking down the sidewalk, hand in hand, nothing in the world to worry over. Like a new breeding division or a dying father. The last thing she wanted to do was add to his stress—to give him a reason to leave.

"No. I don't plan to tell him at all."

Chapter Twenty

Alex knocked softly on the door of his father's house—what used to be his parents' house, and if the doctors were right, would become just a house in three months or less.

Memories hit of his mother's kind voice, his father's praise when one of the boys succeeded. Playing catch in the yard out back, then them cheering from the stands when Alex pitched his first no-hitter. What would happen to the house where he'd grown up after his father passed, too? It'd go to the boys, and none of them would want to live in the house, so what then? It'd sit untouched, growing old and dusty, all the life once in it gone with the death of its owners.

The thought sent a sharp stab into his chest, and he clutched the spot to try to work out the pain before he saw his father. He didn't want to look at him like he was a pity case. If he knew anything about Carter Hamilton, it was that he was no pity case, even when it came to his imminent death.

He knocked once more, then took a step back to leave just as the door opened and there Carter stood, looking even frailer than he had at the meeting weeks before. Had it already been weeks?

"Alex?"

"Hey, Dad, can I talk to you for a bit?"

Carter waved him on in. "Your brothers aren't here, if that's who you're looking for."

"No, I came to see you actually."

This seemed to surprise his father, and Alex wondered if he'd become that son—the one who never called or stopped by unless something was wrong.

They walked out to the back patio, parts of the farm visible from this vantage point. A soft bubbling sound filled the air from the fountain that sat in the center of the nearby garden. Flowers and bushes cradled the flagstone patio, and there was a bench and a table with four chairs for seating. The patio used to be his mother's favorite spot to sit and read.

Once they took a seat at the table, the silence became unbearable. Alex opened his mouth to speak, then shut it again, unsure how to begin.

"How about I start this? I'm dying. And having lost my father, I know that's not the easiest thing to digest." He focused on his son with concerned eyes. "What can I do to help?" It was the most caring statement Alex had ever heard from his father, and he didn't know how to process it.

The well of pain and anger and sorrow in his throat threatened to spill over. "What can you do? Well, you could live, but seeing as how that isn't looking so good, how about what can I do? What would make it better for you?"

Carter thought about it for a moment, then focused back on Alex. "There is one thing."

"Anything. Anything at all I can do."

"Ask Trip to move up the wedding. I can't do it myself. I just . . . I can't. But I'd like to see it, and I don't know if . . ."

"Done."

"But if it's too much trouble, then don't cause a fuss. I know how these things matter to women. I wouldn't want to see Emery disappointed."

"It's no trouble at all. I'll talk to him today. Anything else?"

His father's gaze went to the farm. "Promise me you won't let this place break you. It's broken me. Broken Trip a few times, too." He glanced at his son. "But you were never so stubborn. You could mold and bend, and that flexibility is what's going to take it to the next level. Don't change and I'll know you'll always be successful. That this farm will always be successful."

Alex pulled back, shocked at what he was hearing. "But I thought you wanted me to change. Wanted me to be more like Nick and Trip."

Carter leaned forward and gripped his knees. "I wanted you to find yourself. Whatever that was. That's what I wanted. And I think you have now."

Alex sat back in his chair, this new piece of information weighing

on him. "Yeah, I think I have, too. And I'm sorry you're sick. Sorry I
didn't react . . ." He shook his head. "I'm sorry."

"It's life. Everyone's going to die. My time's just coming a little
early. Make sure to live your life fully, son. You never know whether
yours will come early, too."

"Are you in any pain?" Alex asked, wishing he'd picked up on
some of the signs over the last few months, but the truth was he rarely
saw his father beyond their weekly meetings.

"Not really. Not now. They tried a few rounds of chemo and radi-
ation, but it was already stage IV pancreatic cancer, with a one percent survival rate. I chose to come home, to live my last days here on
the farm, around my family."

Guilt hit in Alex's chest. Around his family, yet there was no one
here. He wondered if Nick or Trip had come by more often. He hoped
they had, but he suspected they, like him, weren't sure how to handle
this. Alex understood why Nick had freaked out at the diner, why he'd
been on edge. It was hard information to carry, and he'd carried it
alone.

"Maybe I should stay here. You know, until . . ."

Carter laughed. "They already have Mama V holed up here. Plus
hospice will infiltrate before long. Not you, too. You and your brother
are on the property. You can get here quickly if something happens."

"Not quickly enough."

"Let me tell you something, son. There is no quickly enough. The
best doctors in the world couldn't save me. You being here won't
do it."

Alex's eyes burned as he stared out over the farm, watching as
mares grazed in a nearby pasture, a few foals milling around their
mothers. He swallowed hard. "Is there anything you need us to handle? B—" He ran a hand over his face, cleared his throat again. "Bur-
ial details. Will. Anything?"

"Our lawyer handled most of it. Nick the rest."

Alex thought of what Becca had said about Nick coming out of
the funeral home and sitting down on the front steps, his face in his
hands. His next visit needed to be to his brother. He shouldn't have
had to carry this alone.

"So, then it's all done."

"It's done."

Alex's eyes cut over to his father. "I'm sorry. For making things hard. For not being here enough. For everything."

"Save your sorrys, son. There'll be a woman one day who deserves them far more than me."

Alex grinned. "Yeah, one day."

"Why not now?"

"Work. My focus needs to be on—"

"Your focus needs to be on the people around you who matter. Business is fine. It's always been fine and it always will be fine. People? Not so much. They need us to be there for them, to pay them attention, to tell them all the things they want to hear. If you have a lady friend who makes you feel good about life, keep her around. Hell, marry her. Time stops for no one, and we have no guarantees."

"Marry her, huh? Were you always so philosophical or is this a new thing?"

Carter shrugged. "Us old guys tend to think we know more than you young ones. And we're right."

Alex laughed. "I'll give you that." His gaze hit his father's. "I don't say it enough, but I'm thankful for what you and Mom gave us. I love you, Dad."

"I love you, too. Now go get that lady friend and bring her back by. I'd like to meet her."

"You would?"

"You plan to marry her someday?"

Alex thought about the question, his future, and then of Kate. She fit into his world so perfectly, into him. He knew he'd fallen for her long ago, but the idea of marriage scared the shit out of him. He'd committed to exactly one thing in his life—the farm and breeding. Adding a second so soon seemed like he was asking for catastrophe to strike. But as he watched his father stare at him with hopeful eyes, he knew there was only one answer to this question. "Yes, I plan to marry her."

The thought thrilled him more than it should. Hmm, marry Kate.

He liked the sound of that.

By the time Alex made the rounds of the various barns on the farm, talked with a few owners, and headed to shower off his day, he was exhausted and ready to grab a beer and fall out on his couch, where he might or might not sleep.

Kate had plans with Emery, so he knew there was no hope of seeing her tonight. That pained him more than it should. He'd gotten used to her sweet smiles and amazing smell. His father's words still hung in his mind, the sureness of his future now so settled that he allowed himself to relax. To hope and dream. It was a change from the Alex of the past, but he liked this change. He could grow used to it.

Alex towel dried his hair and slipped on pajama pants, then went to the fridge for a cold one before plopping down on his couch. All of ten minutes passed before he heard a knock on his front door. For a second, he contemplated ignoring it, pretending he wasn't home or something, but then he noticed that every light in his house was on and the TV, so whoever it was would know that a) he was watching *Arrow*, and b) he was one hundred percent home.

Sighing, he pushed off the couch and managed to make it to the door without falling over, but there was no putting on more clothes. The knock came again and annoyed, Alex called out, "Coming. You can stop killing my head."

He opened the door, expecting Trip or Nick or someone else, here to give him grief about something, but instead Constance Martin, a woman he'd been with several times, stood in his doorway. They had a history of calling the other during a drought or whenever the need arose, and clearly the need had arisen for her tonight.

"Constance."

"I have a few hours before my night shift and wondered if you wanted some company?" She worked at Rudy's at night, which was how he'd met her in the first place. But while a few months ago her offer would have been tempting, he found himself filling his doorway fully to ensure she knew he meant what he planned to say next.

"I don't think so, but thanks for coming by."

"No?" She looked at him through her dark bangs, like he'd turned into an alien overnight. Maybe he had. "Are you seeing someone, then?" She said the words with a bit of a laugh, which grated on Alex's nerves. He wasn't a relationship type, but that didn't mean he was incapable of one.

"Actually, yes."

She stared at him. "Seriously?"

"Yes. Why is that so shocking?"

"I don't know. I guess I think of you as the dessert kind of guy. Not a main course."

Alex didn't know whether to be offended by her words or flattered. "Not anymore."

"Wow, all right, then. I'd be lying if I said I wasn't a little bit jealous. But good luck to you. She's a lucky girl." She rose onto her toes and kissed his cheek. He patted her back before she pulled away, and that was when his eyes locked on a second person in his walkway—this one so angry the red in her cheeks rivaled that of her hair.

"Red?"

"I'm such an idiot." She turned away, and Alex brushed past Constance with a quick "Excuse me" and took off after Kate, but it was no use. She sped away, leaving him and his mistakes in her wake. But he had a car—three actually—and he'd discovered today that Kate wasn't the kind of woman you let go. She was the kind of woman you chased and chased and chased until she realized there was no better man for her than you.

He jumped in his truck and followed after her, ignoring speed limits and seat belts, all thought on this woman who filled his world with such happiness. How hadn't he realized before how much he needed her? How empty his life had been without her? Well, no more. Forget Trip and his judgment. Forget the town and their assumptions. Alex had found the woman he wanted to spend the rest of his life with. Now, he needed to convince her that he was worthy of her forever.

It took a surprisingly short amount of time to reach Kate's house and, as expected, she was already there, no lights on but in the kitchen, and he feared what sugar addiction her seeing him with Constance would have forced her into.

Parking his truck, he walked up the drive, but before he could even knock on the door, it swung open and she stood there, a spoonful of ice cream in one hand, her other on the door. "Look, I don't need an explanation. It's fine. We're not serious, yada, yada, yada. Now, if you could go so I could get back to my—"

But before she could continue, Alex took the spoon from her hand, ate the bite, and then handed it back to her.

"Hey! That was mine."

He stepped inside, edging her back, and closed the door behind him. "You're not having ice cream unless you're eating it with me."

"You were busy."

"Yeah, busy telling her I'm not into that kind of thing anymore."

Kate's eyebrows shot up. "For real?"

"For real."

Kate took another bite of her ice cream, like she needed the distraction so she could think. "What else did you tell her?" she asked, her voice small. "Because she was pretty. Very pretty. I'd understand if you decided to go that way. Well, not understand exactly, but you're a guy, and guys like pretty and—"

"Stop." He pressed a finger to her lips; then, unable to stay away, leaned in to kiss her, but she pulled away.

"I can't. Not if you're doing that. And what was that celibacy talk anyway? Just no sex with me, but sure, fine with anyone else?"

"No. If you'd let me finish—"

"Because I love dancing and laughing and driving in your fast car, but I'm also a woman with needs and—"

"I told her to leave, Kate. I told her that I'm a one-woman kind of man now, and that woman wasn't her."

Her eyebrows hit her hairline. "Oh, yeah? And just who might that woman be?"

Alex took a step now, testing, a smile playing at his lips as he leaned in to her again. "An incredibly sexy redhead who likes to boss me around and act like she doesn't care." He pressed a soft kiss to her lips and whispered, "When I know she does, because I care. Too much for it to be one-sided."

"You do?"

"You have no idea. Things are complicated right now, but being with you is the simplest thing I've ever done. It feels natural—right. I don't want to be with anyone else."

Kate inched closer, then, still hesitant, but he could tell she was enjoying what he was saying. "But you said we should go slow and keep this casual."

"I know. But that was before I fell under your wicked spell. Now there's no breaking free. I'm in."

"All in?"

"All in." His cell buzzed in his pocket, but he had a point to prove here, so he ignored it instead, pulling Kate into his arms and kissing her properly. The phone rang twice more, but each time he ignored it, eager to show this amazing woman just how much she'd affected him. And just how much he wanted to affect her, until she screamed his name again and again.

Taking her hand, he set down her ice cream carton on a side table and led her back to her room, glad to have finally discovered what he wanted out of life. Two things: breeding and Kate. Give him those two simple things and he would be a very, very happy man. And somehow he suspected with Kate on his side the breeding would take care of itself. Just continue doing what he was doing and everything would be fine.

It had to be.

For now, he wanted one thing, and he'd denied himself long enough.

"Alex, should we——"

"Shhh." He pressed his lips gently to hers, then again, because once was never enough with her, and then pulled back to look at her. "Tonight."

Her eyebrows threaded together, and then he gripped his shirt and tugged it over his head, his eyes back on her, heat building in his chest, dropping lower and lower.

"But you said we couldn't."

"I know, but I'm done with that. I want you. I've wanted you since the first time I saw you, and unless you're against it, I'm ready to show you just how much."

She swallowed hard as her gaze dropped to his pants, to the evidence of his need. "You're sure?"

"Never more sure of anything in my life." And then he pressed a kiss to her neck, then her cheek, and suddenly, the growing passion between them boiled over, and they were undressing each other between kisses, lost to anything but the moment and the intensity building, unwilling to remain contained another second.

They slipped under the covers of Kate's quilt and sheets, taking their time to explore all the areas they'd been too careful to explore before. He took his time across her skin, tasting the sweet and salty spots on the curve of her waist, the dip of her breasts, the inside of her thighs, until her hands clenched the sheet, soft moans releasing from her lips, and he couldn't wait any more.

Pulling a condom from his pants, which he'd put there just for this occasion, he rolled it on, and then with one long look at the woman who'd invaded his life, his senses, his everything, he drove inside her, relishing in the tightness and warmth, his nerve endings all sparking to attention, eager for a quick release, but he refused to make this quick.

Pulling back, he pressed his lips to her breast, toying with her nipples, her collarbone, and then, when he wasn't sure he could take it anymore, he went for her mouth, kissing her without restraint, and suddenly he thought maybe this was what love felt like. Maybe it was wild and carefree and full of too many emotions to process. And if so, if this was love, then maybe it was worth taking a chance on after all.

Chapter Twenty-one

Kate read through the lines for their play practice that day, her heart still numb from the night before. She went to sleep cradled in Alex's arms and awoke the same way, a smile on her face, like she'd been dreaming and woke to realize it wasn't a dream at all. This was her reality. She'd finally found her fairy tale, her prince, her happily-ever-after, and the realization made her so giddy she'd found herself drifting off several times during practice, unable to concentrate on—

"Ms. Littleton?"

Her gaze snapped to the stage. "Yes?"

"You were supposed to give us the next line," Greer said, his hands on his hips, like he knew just what her problem was and planned to judge her fully.

She shook her head, but she couldn't shake the smile. "Right. Sorry. Okay, so start at the next to last line."

The stage was already set for the performance, Juliet's balcony behind them, gardens of flowers all around them, both painted on the set and real ones. Kate loved flowers and she loved this play. Loved seeing her kids perform it. Loved watching their excitement at all they'd accomplished. Loved the memories she had with Alex here, him helping along the way.

Loved him. The thought made her smile for the trillionth time that day.

Greer flipped the stapled pages in his hand and turned to Juliet, but where he'd been fully embarrassed before, now he was a pro, his hand already reaching out to take hers. Alex had cured his fear, just as he'd cured hers.

Thoughts of their planned date that night swarmed through her mind, causing her body to buzz with anticipation, until Greer cleared his throat again.

"Ms. Littleton?"

"Yes? Oh, sorry, right, that was perfect." She clapped her hands together and the kids all stared at her.

"I forgot my line. Again."

"Oh." She stopped clapping and crossed her arms. Clearly clapping wasn't the right thing there. "That's all right. Go again."

Juliet spoke up, then. "You seem a little distracted today, Ms. Littleton. Should we give you a break?"

Kate grinned at the sweet girl. "No, honey, I'm fine. But actually"—she checked her watch—"it's time to wrap up. So Wednesday we'll go again, same time."

The kids all scurried for fear she'd change her mind and call them back, and Kate took to cleaning up the auditorium so the janitor would stop glaring at her.

Just as she finished up and closed the door, she noticed Emery's Jeep parked beside her car. She hadn't come in but instead was sitting in her car, her expression full of concern as she nodded along to whatever the person on the other end was saying.

"I know. I know," she said, her voice clear through her lowered window. "But can you try to be easy on him? It happens. I know. But—all right. Yes. Okay. Talk to you later. Love you."

She ended the call and peered over at Kate. "Have you talked to Alex?"

Fear gripped Kate's chest. "No, why? What happened?"

"One of the broodmares miscarried. A McKendricks mare."

"No. I saw them just a few days ago. There has to be a mistake; it—"

"That was Trip on the phone. No mistake."

Worry worked through Kate's stomach. "I need to call him."

"No, don't. He's about to get ramrodded by his entire family. Give him some time to breathe."

"You don't know him like I do. No one is ever there for him. He has to know I'm here."

Despite Emery's insistence that she shouldn't call, she did, only for the phone to ring and ring before going to voice mail.

Everything in her slowed down as she tried not to read too much into this. People missed calls all the time. He could be in a meeting, could be on the phone, could have left his phone in his truck or at his house. But deep down, she knew it was more than that.

"He didn't answer."

Emery nodded slowly. "He's probably just on the phone."

Kate glanced away, unwilling to see the pity she knew she'd find in Emery's eyes. "Yeah, probably."

"I was going to ask if you'd like to go sample food with me for the reception, but if you need to go see Alex, I'd understand."

Kate forced herself to remain calm and look back at her friend. "No, let's go. I'm sure he's trying to figure this out. I'll call him later." But she had a sinking feeling that he'd ignore that call, too.

Somehow avoiding things felt like the better option than admitting that Alex was shutting her out.

"Can we drop my car by my house, then take yours?"

"Sure," Emery said. "I'll follow you over."

Kate tried to calm her racing mind and heart as she parked her car in her garage, then slipped into Emery's Jeep. A part of her had hoped Alex would be there, that he'd be sitting on her front steps, that he would have come to her for comfort as he had after he'd found out his father was dying. But this was different. This was work, and the very reason he'd held off on becoming more with her for all these weeks and months, and now, the day after they decided to take it to the next level, one of his mares miscarries, a loss of hundreds of thousands of dollars.

Growing up on a farm, Kate knew this kind of thing happened. A thousand things could have caused it, and if the mare was healthy, then at least they could breed her again and hope for better results. But then there were stud fees to consider, and who to blame—Mother Nature or Alex—and the McKendricks still had another horse at the farm and were very influential. They could pull their business and ensure few worked with Alex after this. But then, surely Trip's reputation meant more than the McKendricks, but Alex would never want this leaning on his brother in that way. For Trip to fix it. There were more questions than answers, all the while Kate kept eyeing her phone, hoping for a text, something, but the screen remained black.

"It's going to be okay," Emery said as they pulled into a space at the Westshire Country Club, where they planned to have the reception. "Trip will fix it."

"Alex doesn't need Trip to fix anything. He can handle it."

Emery's expression softened. "Of course he can. I just meant—"

"I know what you meant. Trip's the one who can do no wrong and Alex is the one who is forever in the wrong. But he's different from what everyone thinks, and you grew up on a farm, just like me. You know this kind of thing happens."

"It does; you're right. It's just that he didn't answer their calls. That's what has everyone so upset."

Kate's heart stopped. "What did you say?"

"Last night. Dr. Vickers called him several times, the farm even more. He never answered."

"Last night."

"Yes. It's not that the mare miscarried. It's that they feel he checked out, wasn't there to help, to make decisions that might have saved the pregnancy. Likely nothing could have been done, but they'll never know now."

"Oh my God." Suddenly, Kate needed to talk to Alex. She knew what this would do to him, the way he'd blame himself, and she couldn't let him go down that road. Not alone. "Can you take me back home? I'm sorry, but I have to see him."

"I don't know if that's a good idea."

Kate focused on her friend. "Please." Then she closed her eyes and confessed the truth. She was done lying to Emery. "He was with me last night. That's the reason he didn't answer the calls. He was ignoring them to prove to me that he was serious about us, and now . . ." She trailed off, sure that if she continued she'd find herself in tears. *Us.* Somehow that sentiment seemed very far away now. Because not only would Alex blame himself, he'd blame their relationship, and though he'd never admit it, maybe even her. She needed to talk to him before he let his guilt control his life and their future.

"Of course. I'll head there now."

Kate parked her car in Alex's driveway and waited, her eyes on the garage and the truck clearly visible inside. He was home now, and she'd called him again, with another voice mail answer, which meant she had been right before. He was ignoring her. At this point, she might not be able to bring him back to the light, but she had to try. This wasn't just any man. This was *the* man. The love of her life, and she refused to allow him to push her away.

Stepping out of her car, she went slowly down the walkway to his front door and knocked softly. No answer. Her heart hurt, but she refused to leave. Not yet. He would have to tell her to leave. Somehow, she knew she wouldn't be able to let this go unless he said the words.

With one more knock, the door opened, and if Kate thought her heart hurt before, it was nothing compared to seeing the broken man before her. His hair was a mess, his eyes dark, a wrinkled T-shirt and gym shorts completing the look that said he'd given up hours ago.

"What are you doing here?" he asked.

Kate opened her mouth to say she was his girlfriend, she was there to make sure he was okay, but they'd never talked about titles. Now it didn't seem fitting. "I wanted to check on you."

"How—Emery." He shook his head. "Fantastic. So not only is my life shit right now but all the town's going to hear about it."

"She didn't tell anyone else, and I'm not just someone from town."

Alex shot her a blank stare and her stomach dropped, before anger flickered to life inside her, shaking her to her core. "Don't you do that. Don't you dare stand there and pretend this is nothing. You've had a bad day and I get that. I do. But relationships are about seeing the other person through the good and the bad. Don't push me away now. We've had too much good to let a little bad ruin it."

"A little bad? A bad day?" He glared at her, his own anger taking over. "You think I had a bad day? Our number-one client is talking about pulling, forget that we just lost a three-hundred-thousand-dollar foal, or that because I didn't answer the phone last night to make a decision on the mare, we may lose her, too. Trip pulled me from breeding, despite the fact that we're brothers and co-owners of the farm. And then, to add icing to the shit that is my life, my father had nothing at all to say about any of it. Which just proves what a messed-up job I've done. If there was anything to be done, he'd do it. He'd explain to me how to fix this. But no. Nothing."

"Maybe he's not saying anything because he knows you can figure it out on your own."

"Do you hear yourself?" He tossed his hands in the air. "A foal is gone, his mother well on her way. There's no bouncing back from this."

"But—"

"No, there's no rationalization here. It's over."

Kate reached out to him and he flinched back. "Let me be here for you. Let me help you through this."

"There's no helping me through this."

"There is. We can talk, figure out what to do next. We—"

"I don't need you to do that."

Her gaze landed on Alex, his arms crossed, his expression hooded. "You don't need me here or you don't want me here?"

He swallowed, looked away, then back at her. "Both."

"You're really going to do this. After everything, you're going to bail."

His jaw ticked as he held her gaze. "That's what I do. I screw up everything I touch. That much is easy. The succeeding part, not so much. So I'm done."

"You're giving up."

"I have no choice."

"Bullshit. You could fight. You could push past this and come out ahead. You could tuck away your ego and try. Then maybe you'd fail, but you'd try again. You don't give up. You never give up."

"No, *you* don't." He pointed at her, anger raging back to life like a fire that refused to die down. "You walk around with your supportive family and set career, but it's not so easy for the rest of us. It's exhausting being around someone so perfect, when you know deep down you'll never deserve them."

"Alex . . ."

"It was time anyway."

Kate drew a rattled breath, blinking hard to keep from crying, but still, her eyes burned so badly she wished she could close them again without the risk of a lone tear falling. "You're a coward. And when you wake up one day and realize it, I'll be gone." She looked at him then. "I'm the one person who loved you for you, who believed in you."

He stared at her, a flicker in his eyes the only hint that her words had hit home. Otherwise, he looked like a stranger to her, not at all like the man who'd been in her home, in her bed, not twenty-four hours before, professing how much she meant to him.

"I don't know who this person is." She motioned to him. "But when the real Alex returns, remind him that we all have bad days. It's how we push through them that defines us."

Then she turned and shut herself back into the security of her car. She made it all the way to the ornate Hamilton Stables gate before a sob broke free and she burst into tears.

Chapter Twenty-two

Alex awoke the next morning with a headache that had nothing to do with alcohol and a hole the size of Texas in his chest. No wonder so many men refused to commit or settle down. The moment you did it, your heart got ripped in half, and it suddenly became a lot harder to be the man you'd once been.

But despite all the mess with Tyrant Queen's miscarriage, she was all right, and after a lengthy conversation with Dr. Vickers and the McKendricks, everything was calmer. They weren't pulling business— yet. And now he had one more task to do that couldn't be delayed another day.

He forced himself into the shower, then dressed in a hurry and grabbed a cup of coffee on his way out. He knew Trip would be down at the track this morning, running a new colt he'd been working the last few weeks. With a deep breath and a dose of courage, he hopped in his golf cart and drove around the winding roads toward the track.

The day was bright, the sky hopeful, no sign of rain in the forecast. Days before, he would have called Kate, asked her to join him for a boat ride on the Cherokee. Enjoy the beautiful day. But everything was different now. He'd gotten lax, and because of it, his career had suffered. He couldn't make that mistake again.

Alex parked by the track, and sure enough, Trip stood just outside it with arms crossed, watching the exercise rider run the colt.

"Hey," Alex said as he neared, which resulted in nothing more than a grunt from his brother. "Look, be pissed off at me all you want, but miscarriages happen. Foals die. It happens. Mares die. Colts die. This business has no guarantees. You of all damn people should know that."

"It isn't about the foal. It's that your job is to know what's happening there and they couldn't get you on the phone. You've yet to admit why, so I can only assume the worst. I trusted you. This entire farm trusted you. And you let us down."

Alex's jaw clenched, but he refused to drag Kate into this. He feared Trip would, intentionally or not, link Kate to what happened, and he didn't want Kate having issues with her best friend's husband. "I said I had my phone off. It was an accident."

"But you weren't at home."

"So? Do I need to wear a tracker so you know where I am all the time? I said I was sorry. I said I'd be more careful next time. I've settled things with the McKendricks."

"No, you haven't. They called an hour ago and are still undecided on sending their two new broodmares. They want to see what happens with Lockley first. We've broken their trust."

Alex felt his already volatile stomach roil, and it took effort to keep from throwing up. He'd never been one to handle stress well, preferring to flee. But while he refused to bring Kate down his destructive path anymore, she'd been right about one thing last night: he had to push through this. And he would. Even if every step was more painful and harder than the last. He'd push through.

"I'll talk to them again."

"No," Trip spit back. "*I'll* talk to them. I'll fix this. Like always."

Once again Alex had to fight not to tell his brother off, but he reminded himself he wasn't here for himself. "Listen, I'm not down here to talk about all of this. Dad asked me to do him a favor, so here I am."

At that, Trip's arms dropped and he turned. "Did something happen?"

Alex shook his head. "I don't think so, but I think it's worse than he's letting on. He asked if you could move the wedding up. He doesn't think he'll make it to August."

"Christ." Trip's head dipped down, and for a moment, Alex wanted to comfort his brother. But then, maybe Trip didn't want comfort from him of all people right now. He had a fiancée for that, and Alex had who? Nobody, because he'd pushed away the one person who meant something to him.

"I know. Do you think we can figure something out?"

"How long?"

Alex thought of his father's pale skin, sunken eyes. "The sooner the better. We should try for some time in the next few weeks."

Trip stared out over the track. "How about this weekend?"

"Can you manage that?"

"I could if we have it here. Have Annie and Patty make the food and the cake early. They won't mind. Then call in a few favors with Mayor Phillips to get chairs and whatnot. I don't want this stressing Emery out. So maybe I'll just call Kate."

"No, don't."

Trip's gaze shifted back to his brother. "Why not?"

Alex stared back at him, unsure how to answer without giving away what had happened.

"You got involved with her anyway, didn't you? And what, now she doesn't want anything to do with our family?"

"No. I meant let me call her. We're friends."

"All right. Call and ask if she can help coordinate with Annie and Patty. I'll take care of the rest. Don't tell Emery a thing."

"Are you going to cancel the August wedding?"

"No. I'll let her make the call after this weekend. If she wants two, she can have two. I won't take that away from her."

Alex watched his brother, curious when he'd become the great man who stood before him. "You're a good man. She's lucky to have you."

Trip's gaze swung to his brother again. "Thanks," he said, but he didn't say it back to Alex, causing the pain in his chest to expand still further. He wondered if he would ever be the kind of man his family could respect.

"All right then, I'm going to call Nick."

Trip nodded to him, his thoughts already turned inward, and Alex set off back to the golf cart, hoping his father's death wouldn't destroy their family for good.

The drive to Kate's proved to be too long and yet far, far too short. He knew what he needed to say, but the words he felt wouldn't change anything. He'd given his all into breeding and still he'd failed. How could he bring Kate into the mess that was his life? She was pure and good from smile to soul. A person like that deserved easiness and structure, not someone like Alex.

Parking outside her house, Alex made the trek up to her front porch, remembering the kisses they'd shared outside her door, neither able to wait until they were inside. How was he going to go on without feeling her lips on his? Her warm hand on his chest first thing in the morning?

He knocked twice on the door and stood back, balancing on one foot to brace himself for the attitude that was sure to come, the *what are you doing here* or *get off my front porch*, or an *I hate you, stupid bastard*. That one might be extreme, but at this point anything seemed possible. But instead, she peeked out the door, then opened it wide, her eyebrows threaded together. "What happened? Are you okay?"

Her care for him after he'd treated her so badly nearly knocked him to his knees. He would never, not in a million years, deserve this woman.

"My father's health has taken a turn for the worse. He requested Trip and Emery move the wedding up, so Trip agreed to do it this weekend, but he doesn't want Emery to know or worry. He was hoping you could help."

Kate reached out to him and took his hand, the move so selfless after all he'd done, it shattered his heart. What was he thinking, pushing her away? "I'm sorry. I'll do anything I can to help. What does he want me to do?"

Alex wasn't listening to her; his eyes were on Kate's hand, still in his, and how it was the first time since he'd heard about the miscarriage that he felt whole. "Kate . . . can we talk?" His eyes lifted, and she pulled her hand away, leaving cold where there had once been warmth.

"No." Her gaze dropped for a moment, like she had to build up enough strength to look at him again. Alex wished he could deck himself. How could he have broken her like this? "What does Trip need me to do?"

"I just wanted to—"

"I said no," she said, her voice harder this time. "You said plenty already, and I'm trying here. I really am. But I can't do both. I can't wish for something with you and be there for your family. Right now, every part of me wants to scream or cry, but this isn't about me. I know that. And I'm willing to tuck away my hurt to help, but not if you keep looking at me like that and trying to have conversations that are bound to go nowhere. Just don't. Please."

Alex took a step back, nodding in assent, though he couldn't find the words to tell her that he would let her go. In his heart, he'd never let her go.

"Now, can you tell me what Trip needs me to do for the wedding or do I have to call him myself?"

"No, I'll tell you. He wants you to talk to Annie and Patty to set up food and the cake. Handle making sure her dress is ready to go, and yours and her cousin's. He said he'd handle the rest."

"Should I talk to Emery about it or not? I think it'd be best if we didn't tell her until right before. She's a planner, and though she'll want to do this for Carter, it'll stress her out. Plus the other wedding . . ."

"Trip didn't want her to know, and he said he'd give her both weddings if she wanted. This one for Dad, and then the full wedding in August."

Kate's face filled with awe. "Wow, he's amazing."

Alex swallowed hard. "Yeah . . . he is."

"I didn't mean . . ." Kate's gaze lifted back to his and he waved her off.

"I know. It's just true. Anyway, thanks, I've got to go meet with Nick to go over some details about Dad."

"Okay."

He dropped his shades back over his eyes, else he'd reveal how hard it was for him to walk away from her right then. "Call me if you need anything? Anything at all."

She nodded. "I will."

But he knew she wouldn't. He'd broken her trust; the one person who'd deserved everything, and he'd let her down. Somehow he knew this failure was the worst of his life.

Chapter Twenty-three

K ate knocked once and pushed through the front door at Trip's house and on to the master bedroom where Emery was getting ready. She'd thought through every detail of this wedding for her friend, and though the weather had called for showers, God had blessed them with sunshine and warmth, and a gentle breeze keeping everything cool. And now she needed to keep Grace Carlisle, Emery's mother, relaxed so Emery could get married without losing her mind.

"Got it," Kate said as she swept into the bedroom. Emery turned immediately, her eyes pleading.

"Thank God. Hurry and play it."

Kate dropped Emery's iPod into the docking station on Trip's nightstand and shuffled through until she found the song. The song Emery had talked about playing on her wedding day since she was eight years old, and she and Kate would pretend to be brides and grooms. "Chapel of Love" filled the room, and Emery released a slow breath. She rose from her chair and Kate smiled. Then it was all dancing and fun. They began singing together as they had all those years ago, Emery relaxing more and more with each twirl and spin. Finally, the song came to an end and she grinned over at Kate.

"I love you, you know that?"

Kate grinned. "I do. And I love you, too."

Then Emery's face fell, and she took a step toward Kate. She was only wearing her undergarments, a strapless bra that went down over her ribs and a slip that looked like something you'd see in *Gone with the Wind*.

"Are you all right? The Alex situation . . ."

Kate swallowed and looked out the bedroom window. The sun

was still shining, the sky was still blue. She'd told herself she'd survive this heartbreak one day at a time. "I will be."

"I could kick his ass for hurting you."

Kate laughed, knowing full well Emery would try if Kate prodded her. "Not in that thing. I don't know how you'd even lift your leg."

Emery's gaze fell to the skirt/slip contraption. "Seriously? Why couldn't I just wear the dress without it?"

"Because you're a lady and you're expected to act like one." Kate and Emery turned to the door to find Emery's mother had returned, a glass of wine in hand despite the early hour. The wedding was on for one, which meant they had twenty minutes max to finish getting dressed and head to the ceremony.

Grace came over to kiss her daughter, then left them alone at Emery's insistence. When Kate had her in her dress, she directed her to stand in front of the long mirror, and Emery gasped, tears filling her eyes.

"No, no. You can't cry. You'll make your face melt off."

Emery laughed. "It's just so real, isn't it?"

"Are you sure about August?"

"Yeah. This is my wedding day. I feel it, ya know? And I've wanted to marry Trip for so long I just want to be Mrs. Trip Hamilton. The rest is trivial."

Kate hugged her friend. "You're a good person, you know?"

Emery kissed her cheek. "You're better."

Doubtful, Kate thought, but being good didn't do her any good anyway. Annie slipped into the room then, her gray hair swept into a low bun, a smile on her face and tears in her eyes. "Goodness, honey, you look beautiful," she said, kissing Emery's cheek. "Now, they're asking for y'all. Try not to trip on anything or pass out." Then she kissed Kate's cheek as a hello and swept from the room.

Kate glanced over at Emery. "Ready?"

"I am."

They stepped outside to a still bright sun and blue sky, and Kate thought even God couldn't deny Emery this happiness. She'd suffered too much and deserved it. "Golf cart or my car?" Kate asked, glancing between the two options.

"Car. I don't think my train will fit on the golf cart."

"You realize I drive a Prius right?"

"Good point. But at least we can shove it in without worry of it getting dirty on the way over because it dragged in the dirt."

Kate clicked the Auto Unlock on her keys. "Good point. Let's go." She helped Emery into the car, draping her train around her as delicately as possible. Then, with one more look at her best friend, Kate backed out of the driveway, on her way to the expansive field beside the track, which they'd purposely chosen so they could get photos at the track after the wedding.

A white canopy completed the look, with chairs split by a cloth white aisle and more flowers than she had ever seen in one location. The string quartet they'd tracked down was already playing, the music floating in the air, and then came "Canon in D," and Emery's cousin, Vanessa, then her turn to walk. Kate waited until Vanessa was down the aisle before following, her gaze fixed on the end of the white carpet runner, though she could feel Alex's eyes on her.

She slipped into the space right next to where Emery would stand and finally allowed her eyes to lift. They immediately connected with Alex. He didn't smile at her or allow his eyes to trail down her as they normally would. Instead, his gaze penetrated through her, filled with too many emotions to process, too many to take in at that moment. Kate looked over at Nick, then Trip, who was smiling so big she couldn't help smiling in return. Then the quartet switched to the "Wedding March," and all eyes turned to the end of the aisle, to Emery walking with her father, and though Kate had seen her just moments before, she looked more beautiful than she'd ever seen her before. Her eyes were shiny with tears, threatening to fall, her smile resolute and pure, so very in love that nothing could tear these two apart. Kate hoped Emery would feel that way from now until she left this earth for heaven, a lifetime of love.

Trip took Emery's hand like he never wanted to let go, and once again, Kate found Alex watching her, a look on his face that said he was sorry, he'd never hurt her again, and on and on and on. But she'd trusted him once before only to have him land her in the dirt. She didn't want to take that chance again. Besides, some stallions could never be tamed. Maybe Alex was one of them. Maybe he couldn't be the man she needed him to be, even if he wanted to be. Even if he tried.

Pastor Reagan set into the discussion of the importance of marriage, the reasons, the care, then he began the vows, and Kate had to

bite her lip to keep from crying. She wanted to say these vows someday, wanted to gaze across at a man who loved her, who would fight
his innermost demons and be a good man from that first day until the
last.

Without thinking, she peered back up at Alex, and he shifted in
her direction, like it was killing him to stand that far away from her.
But the distance was nothing now. Closing it wouldn't fix their problems.

The service ended with an embarrassingly long kiss from Trip
that had Emery laughing as she pushed him away, then they set off
for the second white canopy. It brimmed with trays of food and a small
stage at the front where one of Emery's favorite local bands was already setting up to play. A makeshift dance floor had been situated
just before the stage, and Kate thought, like many weddings before,
she might never actually get a chance to use it.

But then the band announced the dance with the wedding party,
and Alex took her hand before she could argue, walking her to the
dance floor to join Trip and Emery, Nick and Vanessa.

"I'm sorry," Alex whispered when they began dancing, the song
slow and sweet, the kind of music played for first dates and first
loves.

"I know."

"But you won't forgive me."

"Would you?"

Alex considered her and shook his head. "No. But you're a better
person than I am."

"I'm not," Kate said, growing frustrated. "You're the second person to tell me that, and let me just clear the air. I'm not. I have horrible thoughts and feelings all the time. I want things I have no reason
or right to want. And I am so sickly jealous of my best friend right
now that it's killing me. I want happily-ever-after, I want forever. I
want to know the person beside me would protect me through and
through. But that's not my story." Her bottom lip trembled and she
clamped down on it. She told herself she wouldn't cry here. This was
Emery's day, and she wouldn't be anything but supportive.

"See, that's where you're wrong. You can be all those things and
still be a good person. It isn't our thoughts that define us as good. It's
our actions. And yours are gold."

"Maybe. But that didn't help me keep the guy, did it?"

"Kate, please—"

"The song's over." Kate stepped away from Alex to clap for the band, then walked away to allow Emery to dance with her father and Trip with her mother, because his was no longer with them. Then Emery reached out to help Carter stand and walked him to the dance floor, his body so clearly frail that he looked like a ghost of himself. Everyone watched in silence as they danced, Carter smiling wide. Like he'd gotten his final wish and was okay for God to take him now.

The sight of it hit her square in the chest and she peered back over at Alex to see him gripping the back of a chair, like he needed it to stand, and though she was angry at him and he'd hurt her more than anyone else dared, she walked over and helped him sit down, then went to grab both of them a plate of food.

"Eat. It helps."

He nodded to her, and she took the seat beside him, eager to stuff herself with Annie and Patty's amazing food in hopes of closing the hole in her heart. At least for one night.

Alex's face creased in agony as he watched his father attempting to dance, clearly exhausted. "I should go help."

"No." Kate placed her hand on his forearm, and his gaze fell to her hand, then up to her.

"I'm scared. For him . . . for us."

"I know."

"How do you say goodbye? How do you find the words to say how much someone means to you?" He blinked hard, and Kate's already fragile heart clenched, matching his pain.

"I think the best we can do is love the people we care about when they're here. Talking about him leaving won't make his time any easier. So talk about what makes him happy. Share memories. Love him. That's all that matters now."

"I'll never get over us."

Kate's vision blurred, her emotions bubbling up. "Neither will I."

Chapter Twenty-four

Alex's hands shook as he worked his gray tie through his fingers, crossing and tucking, until he'd formed the knot his father had shown him when he was just a boy. His father had shown him . . .

He tightened it to his collar, immediately feeling like all his oxygen had been cut off, then slipped on his black suit jacket and stared at his reflection, the weight of loss so heavy on his chest he wondered how he stood at all.

It had been three and a half weeks since Trip and Emery's wedding, and each day his father had deteriorated more, until finally, the brothers made the impossible decision to take him off life support, living causing him more pain than dying. And though that had taken more strength than he felt he had, this was harder. He knew as soon as the funeral was over, he would never see his father again, and then both his parents would be gone. The thought caused his throat to tighten, his eyes to burn, but he knew his brothers, especially Nick, would need him today. So he climbed into his Vette and set off for the funeral home.

Carter was the one who'd found the car for him, convinced him to buy it, showed him what to do as a teenager. Told him a man should be able to fix a car, so Alex learned the skill. Like so many others, he'd learned because his father wanted him to be the best man he could be. Because Carter was that kind of great man—the greatest man. And now he was gone.

The day was dark for two o'clock, the air heavy with humidity, the threat of rain looming. Alex said a silent *thank you* to God for giving them darkness on a day like today instead of light. He didn't think he could face a sunny day. Not today.

Alex parked outside the all-brick funeral home, which actually resembled a house. He wondered if they'd built it to look this way, or if the original Dawson who founded the funeral home had decided just to make use of his basement. These sorts of thoughts were running rampant in his mind, all in an effort to avoid those dangerous thoughts that threatened to cripple him.

Walking inside, he found Trip and Nick sitting outside the chapel, not speaking, both staring at the doors like they weren't sure how to open them.

"Come on," Alex said. "We should make sure . . ." He eyed the doors, then his brothers. "Flowers or something?"

"Emery handled them," Trip said.

"Music's in order or something?"

"The funeral coordinator."

"So then, all that's left is to . . ."

"Go inside." Nick gripped the arms of his chair, his eyes clearly bloodshot, and Alex had a new appreciation for him that he didn't try to hide it. Trip appeared as emotionless as ever, but Alex knew his brother and could tell he was hurting, too. The creases at the corners of his eyes, the way he slouched. And Alex knew he'd have to be the one to open the door.

Taking a step toward it, then two, he heard the door to the funeral home open, and Kate walked inside, the sight of her washing over him like a warm fire on a cold, cold day. Alex released a relieved breath, his eyes burning for the hundredth time that day. He sucked in a ragged breath. "Kate . . ." And she rushed for him, taking his hand and reaching for the door, opening it, then waiting for Trip and Nick to follow before stepping in after them. The chapel was already full, all the farm staff taking over much of the seating area, but also people from Triple Run and Crestler's Key alike, plus many, many people from Hamilton Industries and then a wealth of connections in horse racing who knew Carter's name and wanted to pay their respects.

By the time the brothers took their seats in the front pew, the place was packed, not a single seat available, many standing in the back, and Alex smiled a bit. Carter would have been thrilled to see so many people there. To know he'd touched so many people's lives.

Kate hugged Emery once she saw her, then started away to stand in the back, but Alex grabbed her hand. "Stay with me. Please." His voice broke midway through his plea, and he thought she might say no, she couldn't, but instead she nodded and followed after him into the pew. Thank God for Kate. For placing her in his path, for making her be a better person than him, for allowing him to fall in love with her so deeply. Because though he felt like his heart was splitting in two every time he saw her, he also felt breathless and alive, something he'd never experienced before. Now, he found himself wondering why he'd pushed her away. Why couldn't he be the man to love and care for her, to stand beside her for the rest of her life?

She'd told him no before, at the wedding, but that was mere days after he'd said the single thing he regretted most in his life—that he didn't need or want her, when all he ever wanted or needed was her. Forever her. Weeks had passed now, and maybe through time her heart had healed a little. Maybe he could try again. And if that didn't work, try again.

He remembered his father's words about love and marriage and asking to meet Kate. He wished they could have met, even if Kate never forgave him. Alex would always love her.

His thoughts cleared as the service began, talk of his father and his accomplishments, and instead of feeling like he wanted to break down, he felt proud and motivated. Carter Hamilton had lived a full life. From military service to business successes to smart investments in real estate and, with the help of Trip, carving the Hamilton name into horse racing, he was a man to admire and revere. Alex wanted to be that kind of man. He wanted to end his life knowing he'd touched the lives of others. That he'd been more than just one man.

Gripping Kate's hand tighter, he swallowed hard and set his mind to his plan, his head tilting back to look at the ceiling as they closed the casket and then the brothers took their place as pallbearers with Clark and some of the other men from the farm. A knot formed in his stomach as he remembered his father's words to him about being himself and living fully.

He was ready to try again. Failure would come, but eventually the cards had to fall in his favor. He just needed to be patient and have the right team on his side—beginning with Kate. Now if only he could think of a way to win her back.

Alex found himself sprawled out on his couch hours later, a beer in hand, exhaustion taking over from countless hours of people and food and thanking people for their kind words. Now he was ready to mourn his father's death by himself, but while he felt sad, he didn't feel like shedding a tear. He felt like doing what his father had asked him to do—to try to be true to himself. He wanted to live for his father now. But how?

A knock on his door startled him from his trance. With great hesitation, Alex pushed off the couch and to the door, but of all the people he expected to find on the other side, it wasn't his brother.

"Have a minute?" Trip asked.

Alex waved him in. "Nothing but time."

Trip walked into the house and sat down on the couch, his hands threaded together. He'd changed from his funeral gear to his usual jeans and flannel shirt, despite the heat.

"I owe you an apology. More than an apology really, but I'll start with that. I'm sorry." He lifted his gaze to Alex. "For second-guessing you all the time. For the miscarriage. For Kate."

Alex straightened, then dipped into the kitchen to grab them both cold beers. "I'll take it for the first, maybe even the second, but not Kate. That was all me, man."

"I don't think so. And I talked to Dr. Vickers. He said Tyrant Queen would have miscarried no matter what. You being there wouldn't have changed a thing. The only reason they kept calling you was to be sure he didn't make a decision you wouldn't have wanted him to make. But we both trust him enough to run the show without us assholes messing him up. I realized I would've told him to do whatever he needed to do, and so would you."

Alex passed over the beer and sat in the chair to the left of his brother, elbows on his knees. "I don't know. I should have gotten the call. Been available."

"You were with Kate, weren't you?"

Nodding slowly, Alex took a long pull of his beer. "I was trying to prove a point to her. That I could be serious and focused and committed. So for one hour I focused on her, ignored my phone, everything but her. And then this happened."

"But she's not the reason it happened."

Alex's gaze cut over at the words. "I know."

"Do you? 'Cause if you do, then why did you end things?"

"In the moment, I think I wanted to protect her from the disaster that is me. I didn't want her to grow more attached and then get hurt."

"That's not how love works, brother. You have little choice about how hard you fall, and all you can do is hope you fall for a good person."

"Yeah, well, she didn't."

Trip focused on his brother. "Actually, I think she did. I think she fell for a good person who's never been given the chance to be great. Well, I'm done with that. All we've got is each other and Nick now to represent the Hamilton name and continue to help it thrive. I was the one who made a mistake here, not you. I should have pulled back and let you do whatever you wanted to do. Handle the McKendricks however you wanted to handle them. Trusted you. I'm sorry for that. You're the breeding manager. Grow it."

"You still think I'm the best man for the job?"

"I think you're the only man for the job. You have a gift for it, and I think this time next year we're going to be training champions. But I gotta tell you, from experience, none of that is going to make your life feel complete."

Alex looked up. "What do you mean?"

"I had success before Emery. Countless trophies. Everyone knew my name. And I was miserable. What I'm saying is that success isn't going to bring you happiness. Maybe for the short-term, but not forever. Not like Kate."

"Kate?"

"You love her. I saw it on your face when we were all at the track the other week, the way you couldn't stop looking at her. And I know how scary that shit can feel, but it gets easier, and with her beside you, I think you can take this thing all the way."

"Love, huh?" Alex let the word settle over him, each second confirming what Trip was saying. He did love her. He loved her more than he'd ever loved anyone. Far more than he loved himself, and it was time he put himself out there for her. Fought the hard fight in order to win her.

"So what do I do?"

Trip stood and clasped his brother on the back. "Beg for forgiveness for being an ass, and then you tell her. All out, emotions visible for all to see, tell her."

"What will she say?"

"No clue. But odds are on you."

Chapter Twenty-five

Kate stood stage left, watching with pride as the auditorium began to fill up, each person in attendance carrying one of the fans the class had made. Already the play was a hit, and it hadn't begun yet. Her students had worked so hard for this, and despite the misery in her chest, she was happy for them. For herself. It was no small feat to get them to this point.

The lights flashed overhead, signaling that the play was about to start, and Kate clenched her fists, her nerves taking over. Until the first group took the stage, read their lines perfectly, then the next and the next. Before long, she relaxed, watching in awe at these little eight-year-olds and their emotion and care with the storyline. They were bold and hilarious, moving and sweet. They were everything she hoped they would be and more.

The set behind them shined vibrant and held memories of them painting, and of Alex working every Saturday for weeks to help them build it. She wondered if she'd missed the mark with him, if a person could be both kind and reckless. If a person could love you but not want you. That thought hurt the most, because she'd thought that night at her house, the night of the mare's miscarriage, he was trying to tell her that he loved her. That he was committing to them and their journey.

But then, if one slip could cause him to push her away so easily, maybe it was all for the best. What would happen if they were married and something happened? But then, this was Alex—the thought of being married to him was as outlandish as hoping he would have shown up tonight.

A part of her felt sad that he hadn't come. He'd helped so much, she'd hoped he would find pride in seeing it all come together, but then she'd been foolish when it came to Alex in more ways than one.

Dropping her head to peer back down at the script, she read the next lines—Act 2, Scene 2—her favorite part of the play and the part she'd worried would bring her to tears. The small stair step was there, just before the balcony, but there was no Juliet. Kate glanced around frantically, searching without luck for her star performer, and suddenly she realized Greer had disappeared, too. The crowd began to whisper, clearly thinking what she was thinking—where the hell did everyone go?—and just as she started to turn back to see what was going on, a horde of kids stormed her from behind, pushing her toward the stage.

"Stop—this isn't—I—" But then she stood in the spotlight, a full audience staring at her as she fumbled for her headset. "Someone figure out what's going on," she said through clenched teeth. And then, just as she'd decided to apologize to the crowd, someone else appeared on the stage, dressed in tights and puffy clothes. But it wasn't Juliet, or even Greer.

It was Alex.

He nodded for her to go to the stairs, and she shook her head, and he pointed, and she shook her head. He smiled brightly, and her eyes widened as he opened his mouth, and she knew just what she would hear next.

"But, soft! what light through yonder window breaks?
It is the east, and Juliet is the sun.
Arise, fair sun, and kill the envious moon,
Who is already sick and pale with grief,
That thou, her maid, art far more fair than she.
Be not her maid, since she is envious.
Her vestal livery is but sick and green,
And none but fools do wear it. Cast it off!
It is my lady. O, it is my love.
O, that she knew she were!
She speaks, yet she says nothing. What of that?
Her eye discourses; I will answer it.
I am too bold, 'tis not to me she speaks.
Two of the fairest stars in all the heaven,

Having some business, do entreat her eyes
To twinkle in their spheres till they return.
What if her eyes were there, they in her head?
The brightness of her cheek would shame those stars
As daylight doth a lamp. Her eyes in heaven
Would through the airy region stream so bright
That birds would sing and think it were not night.
See, how she leans her cheek upon her hand.
O, that I were a glove upon that hand,
That I might touch that cheek!"

Kate clenched her teeth tighter, her eyes switching from the full crowd to him. "What are you doing?" she hissed.

"She speaks!"

The crowd broke into laughter, and Kate felt her cheeks flush, her entire body lit with embarrassment.

"Alex."

"O, speak again, bright angel! For thou art
As glorious to this night, being o'er my head
As is a winged messenger of heaven
Unto the white, upturned, wondering eyes
Of mortals that fall back to gaze on him
When he bestrides the lazy puffing clouds
And sails upon the bosom of the air."

Kate touched her forehead gently. "This isn't happening." But instead of the words spoken quietly to herself, they blasted out over the auditorium, and that was when she realized her little horde of traitors had mic'd her before pushing her out onto the stage.

Alex took a dramatic hoppity-leap thing toward her, and she shook her head, a grin spreading on her face despite the horror of the situation.

"Are you insane?"

He turned his head to the crowd then, raising his eyebrows and cocking his head. "Shall I hear more, or shall I speak at this?" The crowd burst into laughter again, completely romanced by him. Then he took a step toward her, his eyes locking on hers, and he dropped down on his knees, taking her hand.

"Yes, I'm insane. Madly, blindly, insanely in love with you. So much so that I don't know how I breathed without you. How I woke up every day. How I went about my life. And I don't want to do it anymore. I need you, I love you, and I will do anything in my power to win you back. This isn't my only act, Kate. I want to finish our play, every day for the rest of my life."

Tears sprung to her eyes, and she blinked, looking away to try to pull in her thoughts. This was the man who'd broken her heart, who'd told her he didn't want her, but then her gaze locked on Emery and Trip in the audience, on her parents, all of them with hands clasped together like they were praying she'd forgive him, and the romantic in her surged.

She smiled down at him, trying to swallow her tears, and failing miserably. Trusting him again would be taking a chance, putting herself out there just to get burned again. But wasn't life full of chances? Wasn't any relationship filled with hills and valleys? She didn't know. All she knew was that she'd longed for this man for weeks now, cried into her pillow and prayed he'd tell her all these things. Now he was here, and she was tired of overthinking it. For once, she wanted to take a leap. Literally.

She flew into his arms, nearly toppling him over, and pressed a kiss to his lips, receiving an audible "Awww!" from the audience. Then Alex pulled away and said, "'O, wilt thou leave me so unsatisfied?'"

Kate blinked. "'What satisfaction canst thou have tonight?'"

He brushed her hair from her face, trailing a finger across her jaw, her lips. "'The exchange of thy love's faithful vow for mine.'"

Kate grinned. "I love you. I love you so very much. Forever."

"Forever?"

"Until you force me away."

"Never. I'm yours now, Red. Take me or leave me." He leaned in to kiss her again, just as the kids all raced onto the stage, clapping, the audience standing, and Kate knew she had her fairy-tale ending. She had her prince.

And she planned to never let him go.

Epilogue

Four years later

Alex tried to calm his heart as he stood up in his seat in the grandstand at the Belmont Stakes, his hands and legs and every bit of him shaking so badly he wondered if he'd survive this race.

"Calm down."

"I am calm."

"You're not." Kate reached a hand up to stroke his cheek, kissed him once, then returned to caressing her very large stomach. She was seven months pregnant with their first child, and he'd begged her to stay home, to rest. But she'd have no part of listening to anything he said. Especially today. Any other race and he might have tried a little harder, but this wasn't just any race.

Soaring Red was led into the starting gate, and Alex peered over at Trip, tension etched across his face. "She's going to do it," Alex said, and Trip nodded, but he refused to pull his gaze from the starting gate, from his wife inside, on the mount.

Hamilton Stables had decided to buy Lockley's firstborn foal instead of selling at the sales for the McKendricks, sensing something special in the chestnut colt. Alex didn't know if his love for the horse was because Kate was the one who advised the coupling that produced him or if it was because they'd lost Tyrant Queen's foal that year. Either way, he'd followed that pregnancy like it was his own child, and as soon as Lockley foaled, they were ready. All of them. Dr. Vickers, Trip, Emery, Alex, and of course Kate, at the time his newly-wedded wife. It had taken little effort to convince Trip that they needed to buy the colt.

Now, three years later, and that horse, named Soaring Red after

Alex's first great love, was about to run for the Triple Crown, Emery his rider, after killing it in both the Derby and the Preakness.

If he succeeded, Alex would have produced a Triple Crown champion as his very first bred horse. That alone would guarantee the farm business for a very, very long time. But add to that Trip being a Triple Crown–winning trainer, Emery a Triple Crown–winning rider, and them owning the horse, which was bound to produce seven times his cost in stud fees already, and this was maybe the single greatest moment for the Hamilton family.

The gates flew open and Alex reached for Kate's hand, as he did every race, his breath held as Red fell back to fifth, always a closer. He liked to keep Alex on his toes, just like his namesake, but before long, they rounded the first turn and he surged like a bullet from a gun.

Still, neck and neck with Tiger's Pride, another amazing horse, and Alex feared Red might run out of steam, might grow tired. But then something amazing happened. The horse found new energy, bursting free from Tiger's Pride, one length, two, six.

"Holy shit!" Alex screamed. And then he crossed the finish line and the crowd went crazy. He bent down to Kate and kissed her. "Thank you. This is all because of you."

"No," she said. "This is all you, love. Both of you." She motioned to Trip, and Alex reached out to hug him.

Trip hugged him tight, clear emotion in his voice as he yelled, "We did it!"

We. Not him but *we.*

And Alex knew despite everything, the rough start to their business, losing their father, and all the trials they faced after, that the Hamilton brothers would continue to thrive. With new family, forever friends, and the security of love, they would thrive.

The Hamilton brothers have horse racing in their blood, and their sprawling Kentucky farm is the family's pride and joy. But they've got plenty of passion to spare...

Nick Hamilton has always known he'd take the reins of the family business when his father died, but that doesn't make it any easier when the time comes. Especially with his two siblings tempted by a shrewd offer from a huge corporation to buy Hamilton Industries. Needing advice, Nick turns to his sensible childhood friend, Becca Stark—and finds her suddenly grown-up beauty ignites brand-new confusion, and crystal clear desire . . .

Becca has loved Nick for as far back as she can remember, but she decided long ago that telling him would be a mistake. Stubborn, strong Nick doesn't see her as anything but the tomboy she used to be—or does he? As she helps him untangle his feelings about the farm's future, the familiar bond between them heats into an explosive attraction—and the kind of love that just might take the lead . . .

**Please turn the page for an exciting sneak peek of
Melissa West's next Hamilton Stables romance
SILENT HEARTS
coming in May 2016!**

Chapter One

"Now, that's a heart attack waiting to happen." Becca Stark eyed the overflowing plate before her. The smell of cooked bacon hit her nose, and though she'd given the stuff up thanks to her genetic predisposition to have the cholesterol of a person who ate cheeseburgers with a side of cheeseburgers, her stomach growled. Why couldn't broccoli *taste* like bacon? Or better yet, why not just make bacon healthy?

But in that moment, her stomach yelling at her in starvation, Becca couldn't care less about what was healthy or her cholesterol.

Taking a peek through the diner's service window at Sage Blackson to make sure the cook wasn't watching, Becca reached for the extra plate of bacon he'd set to the side for the next round of orders. But before her fingers could lock around a delicious strip, Sage popped her hand and pointed his spatula at her.

"You remember what the doctor said."

Pouting, Becca crossed her arms. "It's not fair. *You* shouldn't even know what *my* doctor said. I haven't eaten yet today, and I took over the morning shift so Caroline could go to her chiropractor."

Willow, the other waitress on duty, settled in beside Becca and leaned against the counter. "You don't say."

Becca looked around like she'd entered a completely different conversation. Then she remembered this was Triple Run, Kentucky: population three thousand five hundred and eighty-seven and home to at least that many conversations, all happening simultaneously.

"Um, no, I have no idea why she went to the chiropractor, nor do I care. Nor should you. Or you." Becca pointed at Sage because while Willow was a gossip, she had nothing on Sage.

Sage ignored her. "Don't just stand there, woman, hurry up and tell us."

Becca rolled her eyes, but there was no escaping this now.

Willow leaned in conspiratorially. "She threw out her back doing the twisted taco with Mayor Phillips."

"No way," Sage said, shaking his head. "And he's a widower. She should know better."

"What does him being a widower have to do with anything?" Becca asked, then cursed herself for entering this conversation at all.

Sage's turn to lean in closer and peer around. "Them widowers are feisty."

"And how exactly would you know that?"

The fifty-eight-year-old's eyes fell on Penny Lewis by the door, who was every bit of seventy, and suddenly Becca had lost her appetite. Such a shame, too—no one made bacon like Sage.

"And I'm out."

But as Becca took over table three's order, she found she was no longer jealous of the eggs and bacon and grits they were about to enjoy. No, she was jealous of Caroline, which had to be the most absurd thing she'd thought all day. Maybe all week. So what if Caroline had injured herself doing the twisted taco? So what if even Caroline had a better sex life than Becca did? What did it matter?

It mattered because Becca's dating life revolved around the town's belief that she wasn't one of the girls, but rather one of the guys. Or more specifically, one of the Hamiltons. And there was one great problem with that belief—no, two problems.

Problem one: She wasn't a Hamilton.

Problem two (which made problem one super important): She was in love with Nick Hamilton.

Becca might have spent her childhood cutting through the woods behind her house that led to the Hamiltons' farm. She might have helped them toilet paper all of Crestler's Key after they claimed to be the home of horse racing, when everyone knew that title belonged to Triple Run. And she might even have taken their dare to climb to the top of Triple Run Baptist and ring the church bell . . . naked. But none of those things made her a Hamilton.

No, Becca would now and, unless the tides changed, forever be a

Stark—the very opposite of the Hamiltons. The Hamiltons were respectable and civilized.

The Starks had no idea what either word meant.

The Hamiltons ruled not only all of horse racing, but all of Triple Run. They were kings, and though Becca knew all three brothers, knew Nick better than anyone else knew him, she would never really exist in their world. And she was fine with that fact. Completely and totally fine. Now, if only she could convince her heart of as much.

But then her heart had never been safe where Nick Hamilton was concerned.

Becca went back to the counter, grabbed the next order and continued around the diner, smiling and handing out food, until she came to the booth in the back corner where a very pregnant Kate Hamilton was working to slide into the booth, but her swollen belly had other ideas.

"Need some help?"

Kate's head lifted, her face flushed, and Becca had to fight off a smile. "Can you get this baby out of me? Because then yes, I'd love some help. Right this second, in fact."

"Aw, honey, I'm sorry, but I'm no help there. When were you due?"

"Eight days ago."

Becca cringed. She knew from her sister that pregnancy was almost never fun, but certainly not in those final weeks and days. To go past your due date had to rank high on the list of most miserable existence on the planet.

"I'm sorry. Maybe you should be lying down at home?"

"My mama's there with the kids so I could get out for a bit. I'm supposed to meet Alex here, but they were running a new colt this morning, and Nick and Trip were both there to see how he did."

At the mention of Nick, Becca's gaze snapped up. "Nick? I thought he was still out of town."

Since Carter Hamilton, the Hamilton boys' father, had passed away and Nick took over Hamilton Industries, he'd been travelling more often than he'd been home, all in an effort to keep up faith in the company and build new connections. And if Becca knew Nick at all, she suspected he hated every minute of it.

The Nick Hamilton Becca knew wasn't a businessman at all. He was an outdoorsman, who used to talk about fishing professionally and sponsorships, but then he met his fiancé Brit and she died and everything changed.

Now, Kate's eyes sparked and she smiled wide. "He just got home today. Want me to text Alex to bring Nick with him?"

Becca shook her head. "What? No. Not at all. Why would I want Nick to come to the diner?" She had taken to smoothing her apron and checking her long, brunette ponytail, which did nothing more than make Kate's smile widen.

"Whatever you say. But yes, he's home. I imagine he'll call you soon. Don't y'all talk every day or something? He's always saying Becca said this or Becca said that. I bet the man can't make a decision without you."

A smile found its way onto Becca's face before she could pocket it, and Kate turned positively giddy. "You know—"

"Hey babe, sorry I'm late." Alex rushed up to the table, kissed his wife, then pulled back to examine the damage. "Scale of one to ten, how pissed off are you?"

Kate stared at her husband, and Becca had to laugh at the nervousness on Alex's face. She never would have guessed the wildest Hamilton would now be such a worried husband and father. "At you or God? Because right now it's neck and neck. You know I can't get into these booths without your help or a solid crowbar, and I forgot my crowbar at home."

"I'm sorry." He kissed her again and then whispered something in her ear that had her smiling again. "Does that smile mean I'm forgiven?"

"That smile means you're dirty. But yes, forgiven."

Alex released a breath, then spying Becca, walked over. "Sorry, Bec, I didn't see you there. Was too distracted by my imminent death, but looks like I'm surviving another day." Becca laughed, and he kissed her cheek before slipping into the booth across from his pregnant wife, who had pushed the table as far away from her as possible, and still had to sit sideways, her feet stretched out across the booth's seat.

"You talked to Nick yet?"

Becca took out her order pad and shrugged. "No, but I'm sure he's busy."

Alex stared at her, and Kate stared at her, and Becca wondered if she'd gotten some of the maple syrup from the bottle she took Pastor Wilkins on her hand then touched her face or hair and she was now slathered in syrup.

It wouldn't be the first time this had happened.

"Um . . . "Becca glanced around, unable to handle the scrutiny. "Is there a sign over my head or something. What are y'all staring at?"

Alex opened his mouth to speak, but Kate slapped his hand and his head snapped over to his wife instead. "Hey! I didn't say anything."

"That's right you didn't. And we need to keep it that way."

"Say anything about what?"

"Nothing," Kate said. "It's a stupid thing."

Becca felt like she'd entered yet another random Triple Run conversation, but this time, something told her the conversation involved her. "All right."

"It's just—" Alex started again and Kate slapped his hand again. "Good God, woman, stop it."

"Well, we talked about this."

"And I disagreed with where we left it."

"It's not your decision to make."

"No one else's making a damn decision, so might as well be me."

"Stop it."

Becca was genuinely perplexed now. "Guys, I'd love to stand here and try to work out . . .whatever this is. But I have other tables, so if you could get to the ordering part." She smiled, and Kate smiled, but Alex still looked offended at his wife's antics.

Kate handed over her menu without looking at it, like most everyone else in Triple Run. In a town where everyone was a regular, she could almost predict orders before they were spoken. "Three pancakes, scrambled eggs, side of bacon and grits. Oh and toast. And do you have any fresh apple butter or honey?"

Wow, Becca thought. She never would have expected Kate to order quite that much food. Surely it wouldn't all fit inside her, but then Becca had never been pregnant before. Maybe the baby inhaled food the way the rest of us inhaled air. A shudder worked through her, the thought scaring her more than it should. She would have to rethink the whole having a baby thing—the insane hunger coupled with hulk-like mood swings and then the pain of actually delivering made the whole thing seem this side of crazy. But then, Becca didn't even have a husband or boyfriend. The last thing she should be worrying about was a baby.

Focusing back on Kate, she said, "We have both. And homemade cherry jam."

Kate's face lit. "Cherry jam? That sounds amazing."

"It's fantastic on the biscuits."

"Oooooo, biscuits. I'll take those, too. With the cherry jam."

The women both looked over at Alex who appeared both impressed and shocked. "Did you leave anything for the rest of the diner?" But at Kate's glare, he quickly corrected. "Um, I meant to say I'll have the same thing." Then he lowered his voice and added to Becca, "And a to-go box or eight."

Becca laughed and went on her way, but once she was a few steps away, she turned back and caught the couple in a deep conversation, Kate lecturing Alex, forever the teacher, and Alex shrugging her off, forever the free spirit. She started to laugh, until she heard Kate say, "This is Nick's thing. We can't intervene."

"Then he needs to do something. You know as well as I do that he wants her, that she's his match. He needs to tell Becca."

"Shh, keep your voice down," Kate said, just as Becca disappeared behind the counter.

Suddenly the diner was too hot, her skin prickly, her heart too heavy in her chest.

So that was what Alex wanted to tell her, what Kate thought Nick himself should confess. It was inevitable, right, but that didn't stop the pain.

Nick had met someone.

www.ingramcontent.com/pod-product-compliance
Lightning Source LLC
Chambersburg PA
CBHW050731250626
47155CB00005B/1751